"Caroline . . ." Sonny looked at her hesitantly. "I have a really big favor to ask you."

"What?" Caroline smiled at him shyly. "You know I'll do anything I can to help you." Even as she spoke, Caroline reminded herself that her purpose in visiting Sonny at the prison was to tutor him for his high school equivalency exam. There was only one catch—he was the best looking man she'd ever seen in her life.

"Remember my friend Jake I told you about?" Sonny whispered. "Would you take him a note for me?" Sonny looked around cautiously. Then he extended his hand casually across the table and palmed a folded piece of paper into Caroline's hand.

"Sonny, you know I can't do that," Caroline whispered softly.

"Please, Caroline! What's the harm? It's just a note asking Jake to come and visit me."

"Well, okay." Caroline hesitated but relented softly, unable to resist his charm.

It can't hurt, Caroline convinced herself later as she walked back to her dorm. *It can't hurt to deliver a note from one friend to another . . . or can it?*

Other books in the **SUGAR & SPICE** series:

COMING SOON

Janet Quin-Harkin's Sugar & Spice

One Step Too Far

IVY BOOKS • NEW YORK

To Carla Bracale

Ivy Books
Published by Ballantine Books

Produced by Butterfield Press, Inc.
133 Fifth Avenue
New York, New York 10003

Copyright © 1989 by Butterfield Press, Inc. & Janet Quin-Harkin

Library of Congress Catalog Card Number: 88-92936

ISBN: 0-8041-0337-2

Manufactured in the United States of America

First Edition: June 1989

One Step Too Far

Chapter 1

"Hey, Cara, what are you doing sitting out here all by yourself?" Chrissy Madden flopped down on the bench outside the Student Union and glanced over at her cousin.

Caroline Kirby sighed, her pretty features barely discernible in the waning light of dusk. "Just thinking," she replied.

"Well, this is a good place to think." Chrissy leaned back against the bench and looked around with a sense of satisfaction. She still couldn't believe that she was actually here at Colorado University.

If the kids in Danbury could see me now, she mused, thinking of her friends back in Danbury, the Iowa town where she'd grown up. Most of

1

them had stayed behind to work on their family farms.

Chrissy knew she was lucky to have parents who encouraged her to experience new places and new things. They'd even encouraged her to spend the past two years in San Francisco living with Cara and her Aunt Edith and Uncle Richard. That had certainly been an experience she'd *never* forget! And now, although money was tight at home, her parents had insisted she go away to college instead of working for a year or two first as she'd suggested. Getting accepted to C.U. after being wait-listed had been the icing on the cake. *Holy mazoly, what terrific icing.* She thought happily.

Living in San Francisco had been exciting, but it was nothing compared to the excitement of being a real college student!

"I love this time of the day," Chrissy remarked, her voice brimming with the enthusiasm that seemed to be her trademark. "Have you ever noticed how quiet the campus gets at dusk? It's like everyone is resting up from the daytime activities and getting ready for the nighttime fun!" She flashed a grin at Caroline, but it slowly faded as she realized that her cousin wasn't listening. "Cara?"

"I'm sorry, Chrissy. What did you say?" Caroline turned and looked at her expectantly.

Chrissy frowned. It was all too obvious what Caroline had been thinking about. "You're still upset about you and Luke breaking up, aren't you?" she asked softly.

"Yes, that and about a hundred other things," Caroline answered with another deep sigh.

Of course she was still upset about Luke. He'd been the one special guy in her life since she'd met him on a visit to Danbury nearly two years ago. But now their relationship was finished. *And I can't blame anyone but myself for the breakup*, she thought dismally, recalling the fateful road trip she and Chrissy had taken to see Luke at Fort Collins Air Force Academy two weeks ago.

"I should have told Luke about Robert right away." Caroline spoke her thoughts aloud. "Then maybe he wouldn't have been quite so angry."

"You can't keep going over it, Cara," Chrissy said gently. She hated to see her cousin so upset—although why Caroline had gone out with Robert Winston in the first place was still a mystery to her. Robert was a graduate assistant in the music department, and a little stuffy in Chrissy's opinion. *It really is a shame things didn't work out with Luke*, she thought. *C'est la vie, I guess*, she added, using one of the new phases she'd learned in French class.

"So, what are the other hundred things that have you upset?" Chrissy asked her cousin.

"Oh, I don't know, everything just seems to be confusing." Caroline paused a moment and picked a dead leaf off her sweater sleeve. "I thought I had my college life all neatly planned out. I was going to belong to all the 'best' clubs, with all the 'best' kids, and take all the 'best' classes. Now, I feel like everything has blown up in my face. The Music Society certainly wasn't the right club for me!" She paused a moment and even in the semidarkness of twilight, Chrissy could see the dark blush that covered her cousin's face. "How was I supposed to know that just because I went out with Robert a few times all the kids in the Music Society would believe I was sleeping with him?" Caroline covered her flaming cheeks with her hands, anger rising up inside her as she recalled the cruel comments she'd overheard coming from the Music Society members that she'd thought were her friends. And the thing that had hurt the most was that one of the people saying the unkind things had been her very own roommate, Ellis Lattimore.

"Oh, Cara, you don't need that bunch of snobs," Chrissy exclaimed. "Those kids in the Music Society don't have warm, human blood running in their veins, they have ice cold Perrier!"

"That's easy for you to say," Caroline retorted. "You don't have to share a room with one of those snobs. Ellis and I are in the middle of a huge cold war right now. We aren't even speaking to each other!"

"It's too bad you didn't get a nicer roommate," Chrissy remarked. She'd really gotten lucky in getting Denise as a roommate. Both she and Denise came from small towns, and they seemed to be on the same wavelength when it came to just about everything. "Believe it or not, Denise is even a bigger slob than I am!" Chrissy exclaimed.

In spite of her depression, Caroline felt a small smile tug at her lips. "Surely you jest," Caroline teased. "You're probably even messier than Oscar the Grouch and he lives in a garbage can!"

"Okay, okay. So I don't get points for organization and cleanliness," Chrissy agreed, remembering how often her room-cleaning skills, or lack thereof, had been a sore point between the two girls when they had shared a room in San Francisco. "But seriously, Cara, surely things aren't that bad between you and Ellis."

"If things weren't that bad, I'd be in my room doing my thinking instead of sitting on this bench," she replied dryly.

"Could you be assigned to another room?" Chrissy suggested. "Maybe there's someone in your dorm who would switch with you."

"I don't think anyone in her right mind would actually want to room with Ellis," Caroline said, then she frowned thoughtfully. "You know, I did hear a rumor last week that one of the senior girls is transferring. I guess her room would be available."

"Do you know her roommate?" Chrissy asked.

"She doesn't have a roommate, she's in a single room." Caroline shook her head dismally. "The resident advisers probably wouldn't let me have her room, anyway. I'm only a freshman, and Freshman don't normally get single rooms."

"But these aren't normal circumstances!" Chrissy protested. "Just tell your RA that you're living with a cold-blooded, snobbish slimeball, and you've got to get out of that room before she turns you into one of her own!"

Caroline giggled at Chrissy's dramatic tone of voice. "I'll talk to the RA, maybe she will have some suggestions."

"Great! Now that we've solved all your problems, I have a problem of my own."

Caroline groaned. It always seemed as though Chrissy's problems got them both into ridiculous situations.

"Don't start your moaning," Chrissy protested. "It's only a teeny-weeny problem. "What will happen to me if I flunk a class?"

"Chrissy, we've only been in school for a little over a month, how can you already be flunking a class?" Caroline asked in amazement. She knew that Chrissy had less-than-wonderful study habits, but she'd always managed to maintain average grades.

"I don't know," Chrissy said miserably. "But, I can't think why else Professor Pauly asked to see me tomorrow."

"Professor Pauly—isn't he your American literature professor?" Caroline asked curiously.

Chrissy nodded. "He stopped me after class today and told me to come to his office at eleven o'clock tomorrow morning, and he wasn't smiling!"

"You didn't cheat on a test or something like that, did you?" Caroline said jokingly.

"Cara! You know I would never cheat on a

test." Chrissy glared at her cousin. "Besides, Professor Pauly hasn't given us any tests yet. All we've done is read some poetry and short stories, and write a couple of papers."

"How did you score on the papers?" Caroline asked.

"I aced them, believe it or not!" For a moment Chrissy beamed proudly, then her smile slowly fell. "That's why I don't understand what I've done wrong."

"Maybe you haven't done anything wrong," Caroline offered.

"Knowing me, it's got to be something," Chrissy said shrugging. "Oh well, I guess I'll know tomorrow." She stood up from the bench. "I guess I'll head back to my own room. It's getting chilly out here."

"If you think this is chilly, you should feel the atmosphere between Ellis and me," Cara retorted with a rueful smile. "But I guess I'll head back to my room, too."

"Are you sure you're all right?" Chrissy asked worriedly. She knew how Cara sometimes took things too seriously for her own good.

"I'm fine," Caroline assured her cousin, giving her a forced smile.

But once she and Chrissy had parted, Caroline lapsed into the melancholy mood that she'd been in so frequently in the past two weeks.

I'm not fine, she thought as she walked the distance between the Student Union and Fielding

Hall, where her dorm room was located. *I'm upset, and I'm miserable, and I'm confused and I don't know what to do about it.*

Luke—his name came to mind along with a deep pain in her heart. She hadn't meant to hurt him. If only he hadn't found that awful letter in which Robert had claimed to love her. The sad part was that Robert really meant nothing to her. Oh, he'd been fun, and it had been rather exciting having an older man attracted to her, but it had never been anything serious. She bit her bottom lip as she walked through the darkness toward the lights of Fielding Hall. She'd hurt not only Luke, but herself as well. Now she'd lost Luke, and she wanted nothing to do with Robert.

She didn't want anything to do with the Music Society, either. She'd wasted the first month of college thinking she'd found her perfect niche. After all, her mother ran an art gallery and her father was a music critic, so culture was practically in her blood.

But I should have realized from the start that the members of the Music Society are more into the appreciation of themselves than the appreciation of music. Maybe at least Ellis and I can work out a truce or something, she thought as she entered Fielding Hall and headed for room 136.

As always, her eyes lit up appreciatively as she entered the small room. At least she and Ellis had made the room look nice. The matching pale blue bedspreads and curtains were complemented by the wall decor over each bed. Ellis had chosen modern art pictures in blue and peach tones for her side of the room, while Caroline had found some magnificent framed travel posters of France. She sat down on the edge of her bed, grateful that Ellis wasn't in the room. At least for the moment she could enjoy the room in peace. She reached over and flipped on her radio, filling the small room with the sounds of a jazz pianist.

Lying down on her bed, she grabbed her biology book, knowing she had a long chapter to read before class the following day.

She'd been reading for about half an hour when the door to the room burst open. She turned to see Ellis enter the room, looking characteristically stylish in a pair of man-tailored twill slacks and turtleneck, jacquard sweater. Caroline waited for Ellis to acknowledge her presence, but when the petite, dark-haired girl studiously ignored her, Caroline returned her attention to the textbook in front of her.

She grimaced as Ellis noisily scraped back the chair beneath the desk on her side of the room. Her grimace deepened as Ellis turned on her radio, the sounds of rock and roll clashing with the mellow jazz station Caroline had been listening to.

Caroline rolled over and sat up on the bed, staring at Ellis's back. "Ellis," Caroline said, keeping a firm grip on her rising anger. "I had my radio on first. Would you mind turning yours off?"

She watched in disbelief as Ellis reached over

to the radio, but instead of turning it off, her roommate increased the volume slightly. *Okay,* Caroline thought to herself angrily. *Two can play at this game.* She reached over and turned *her* radio volume up, cringing at the cacophony of noise produced by the duelling radios. *This is ridiculous,* Caroline thought as Ellis reached over and boosted the volume on her radio once again. *This is stupid and childish. Not only are we making it impossible for us to study, we're probably irritating everyone in the dorm.* In defeat, Caroline turned off her radio.

Ellis immediately turned her radio down to a normal listening level, then threw Caroline a smug look over her shoulder.

How could I ever have admired her? Caroline wondered in amazement. *She's mean and spiteful, and first thing in the morning I'm going to talk to my RA and see if I can transfer out of this room!*

Chapter 2

Chrissy stood outside the door to Professor Pauly's office, her heart beating a rapid tattoo in her chest. She'd tried since yesterday not to let this meeting worry her, but she couldn't get it off her mind. She'd tossed and turned all night, wondering what she could possibly have done to get her in trouble with the professor. She liked his class and she'd thought she was doing pretty well in it.

Clutching her American literature notebook tightly against her chest, she knocked rapidly on the office door.

"Come in." Professor Pauly's voice came through the door.

Chrissy opened the office door and stepped inside, immediately noticing the middle-aged, balding professor seated behind an impressive wooden desk. "Professor Pauly, I brought my notebook with me in case there was some question about my grades, or the papers I've written. . . ." Chrissy blurted out nervously.

Professor Pauly looked at her with open amusement. "Please, Ms. Madden, sit down and relax." He smiled patiently as Chrissy sat down on the straight-backed chair in front of the desk. "I don't understand why it is that whenever a student is summoned to talk to a teacher, the student always assumes the worst!"

Chrissy grinned sheepishly. Professor Pauly certainly wouldn't be joking around if he was going to flunk her—would he?

"The reason I've called you in here today is because The *Campus Times* is being expanded, and as faculty consultant for the newspaper, I've been asked to recommend someone to write a new column. I would like to recommend you." He looked at her expectantly.

"Me?" Chrissy squeaked in surprise. "Why me?"

Professor Pauly gave her another look of amusement. "I've now had an opportunity to read several of the papers you've written for my class, and I must say, you have an intriguing way of looking at things."

"I do?" Chrissy looked at him in amazement.

"Indeed, in all my years of teaching, I've never had a student who compared the letters of St. John de Crévecoeur to the letters of a boy in Iowa."

Chrissy blushed, recalling the paper she'd written using the love letters she'd received from Ben Hatcher, her old boyfriend from Danbury. She'd been madly in love with Ben when she'd first left Danbury for San Francisco. But after living in the city, Chrissy had found that she'd changed and she and Ben no longer had much in common. They were still friends, but now Ben was going out with Marylou Watkins. *And I've got William!* Chrissy thought, smiling to herself.

"The amazing thing to me was that your paper showed remarkable clarity and insight in comparing the 1700's to the present," Professor Pauly continued. "However, the column we have in mind for the newspaper wouldn't require that sort of critical depth. Actually, you would be writing a social column."

"A social column . . ." Chrissy repeated slowly. She'd gotten herself in so much trouble writing an advice column for her high school newspaper, she didn't want the same thing to happen again. Besides, she always had enough trouble keeping her own life in order. "What exactly would I be doing?" she asked Professor Pauly curiously.

"We'd like you to be a sort of roving reporter, writing about the social activities that take place on the campus." Professor Pauly smiled at her, making his dark brown eyes sparkle youthfully. "Of course, I'd like to see you have fun with the column. Use your imagination. Make it a column that everyone will want to read each week." He rubbed his hand across his bald forehead thoughtfully. "And as an added incentive, you'll get extra credit for doing the column. After all, it will be an example of American literature, won't it?"

"Whew! That's a pretty strong incentive," Chrissy laughed. *It might be fun,* she thought. *I like to write, and a social column wouldn't be anything like the advice column I wrote in high school. And maybe I'll decide I really want to be a journalist when I finish college.* "Okay." She grinned at the professor. "I'll do it!"

"Great!" Professor Pauly smiled brightly and stood up, reaching over the desk to shake her hand. "Welcome to the staff of *Campus Times.* Your first column is due in three days."

Three days, holy mazoly, what have I gotten myself into? Chrissy wondered as she walked from the English building across campus toward her dorm room in Culver Hall. *The only club meetings I've been to here were for the Climbing Club, but there are a zillion clubs around the campus. What am I going to write about first?* Chrissy grinned. Now she would have an official reason to go to all the dances and parties on campus. *I'll be able to meet all kinds of people and do lots of fun things!* With this happy thought in mind, Chrissy entered Culver Hall. Not wanting to wait for the elevator, she ran up the four flights of stairs to her room.

"Guess what?" she blurted breathlessly to her

roommate, Denise, who was sprawled across the bottom bunk bed reading a magazine.

"What?" Denise asked, flipping the page and whistling lowly at an ad featuring a tanned, blond hunk in a skimpy pair of swim trunks.

"You are looking at the new social reporter for the *Campus Times*," Chrissy announced proudly.

"No I'm not, I'm looking at the man of my dreams," Denise giggled, not taking her eyes off the magazine ad.

Chrissy leaned over and studied the male model. "He's not so hot." She grinned. "He's not half as good-looking as William." A soft smile touched her lips as she thought of William Powell, the guy she had met when she and Cara had visited the Fort Collins Air Force Academy two weeks earlier.

"Oh, that reminds me, there's a letter for you on your desk, and the return address is Fort Collins." Denise laughed as Chrissy squealed with excitement and raced for the desk, stumbling over a pile of dirty clothes in the process.

"Why didn't you tell me this was here the minute I walked in?" she said in exasperation, ripping open the envelope with trembling hands. "I can't believe he wrote me already!" She sat down at her desk and opened the letter, reading the words slowly and carefully as if to memorize each one.

"What does it say? Is he madly in love with you? Is he going to quit the Air Force and fly off with you into the sunset?" Denise swung her feet to the floor and sat up on the edge of the bed, looking at Chrissy expectantly.

"Well, not exactly, but he writes that he had a wonderful time when he visited me here last weekend, and he hasn't stopped thinking about me since he left."

Chrissy hadn't stopped thinking about William either. She'd met the handsome, gray-eyed senior cadet at a party in Fort Collins, and there'd been something special between them from the start. They'd spent nearly every available minute together that weekend, and the more Chrissy learned about William, the more she liked him. Then last weekend, he'd come to C.U. to visit her and again they'd had a wonderful time. Chrissy wasn't sure how she knew, but she was certain this was the real thing.

"Have you ever met a guy and after spending just a little while with him, you feel like you've known him forever?" Chrissy asked her roommate. "That's the way it was with William and me. We just clicked right away!"

"Gosh Chrissy, you're so lucky, to have a senior at the Air Force Academy crazy about you." Denise looked at her with a touch of envy, then looked back down at her magazine. "And to have him better looking than this guy." Denise whistled once again.

Chrissy grinned and looked at the ad more closely. "That guy is pretty hot," she admitted, "but I bet he's not as nice as William."

"I could live with nice," Denise said. "At this

point in my social life, I could live with anything!
I haven't had a date for two weeks!" she finished
glumly.

"You're just going through a dry spell," Chrissy
said optimistically.

"Speaking of social lives, what was it you were
telling me about being a social reporter or
something?" Denise closed her magazine with
one last lingering look, then looked at Chrissy
expectantly.

"Oh, Denise, it's going to be great!" Chrissy sat
down on the floor and folded her legs up beneath
her, her blue eyes sparkling with excitement.
"I'm so lucky! Not only do I have a wonderful
boyfriend, I'm also going to be the reporter for
the soon to be most popular column in the
Campus Times!"

What's wrong with me? Caroline thought unhappily, staring at the French literature book in front
of her. Normally she enjoyed reading the literature book, but lately she felt like the whole idea
of majoring in French literature was silly and frivolous. *Like my roommate*, she thought, directing
her gaze toward Ellis.

Ellis sat at her desk, which at the moment was
covered with just about every beauty cream and
lotion known to mankind. She was dressed
impeccably as usual, in a pair of designer jeans
and a silk blouse that had probably cost as much
as three or four of Caroline's nicest outfits.

That used to impress me, Cara thought reflectively. *Money, looks, status—all that used to impress me.* She frowned, watching as Ellis smoothed some moisturizing cream on her face with one perfectly manicured finger. *Like the way Ellis says "linens" instead of "sheets" and always dresses as if she has an audience with the Royal family.* Cara shook her head slowly. It didn't impress her anymore. She knew that if she peeled away the designer clothes, took away the layer of makeup and jewelry, there was nothing left of Ellis. She was about as deep as a rock!

"Where are you headed tonight?" Cara asked cautiously, never knowing lately whether Ellis was going to speak to her or not.

"A bunch of us from the Music Society are going to the Rocky Mountain Club," Ellis answered, not bothering to even look at Cara.

Cara stared at Ellis in disbelief. The Rocky Mountain Club was a café in the basement of the Student Union, hardly the Music Society members' normal stomping grounds.

"What are you doing? Slumming for the night?" Cara asked in disbelief.

"As a matter of fact, we are," Ellis responded coolly. "We thought it would be a hoot to see how the other half lives."

Both girls turned as there was a knock on their door.

"Come in," Cara called, grateful for the intrusion.

"Hi." Connie, resident adviser on Caroline's

floor, stuck her head in the door. "I got a note that you wanted to talk to me, Cara."

"Uh ... yes ... but it wasn't anything important." Cara blushed. It was awkward enough to ask about transferring out of a room because you didn't get along with your roommate, but it was virtually impossible to discuss it in front of that same roommate!

"I've got a few minutes right now. Why don't you come on down to my room?" Connie suggested with a smile.

"Okay," Cara replied quickly. She jumped off the bed and followed Connie out of the room and down the hall.

"Have a seat," Connie said, pointing to a big, overstuffed chair that sat in the corner of her room. "What can I do for you?" Connie sat down on the edge of her bed and looked at Cara with friendly interest.

"Well ... uh ... I was sort of wondering how one goes about transferring to a different room," Cara said nervously. "I don't want to cause any problems, or anything like that but ..." She looked at Connie miserably.

"But you and Ellis are having some problems," Connie finished, smiling at her sympathetically. "I guessed as much."

"Ellis and I just don't seem very well suited for sharing a room." Cara took a deep breath to steady herself, feeling the press of tears behind her eyelids. *This is so childish, to cry just because you don't like you roommate,* she berated herself.

But the past week had been so miserable. She and Ellis were barely speaking to one another, and when they did, it was usually cold and indifferent. There was a constant thick tension in the room that Cara found both exhausting and frustrating.

She gave a small, self-conscious laugh. "I feel like such a baby, coming to you, but I didn't know what else to do. Things have really been difficult between Ellis and me."

Connie nodded with understanding. "Usually the people who make the room placements do a pretty good job of matching up students with similar interests and values, but they occasionally place two girls together who simply can't get along. It sounds like that's the situation with you and Ellis."

Cara nodded miserably. "Things just seem to be getting worse and worse between us. It's gotten so that I hate to spend any time at all in my room."

"Now we can't have that," Connie said. "That room is your home while you're at the university. You should enjoy spending time there." Her smile slowly faded. "Cara, I can't promise you anything. As a general rule, room transfers are automatically rejected. However, in this case, I'll do my best. Knowing Ellis and knowing you, I think you both would feel better if you weren't roommates." She frowned thoughtfully. "We do have a senior girl leaving to get married and as far as I know, her room is going to be empty.

Perhaps something could be worked out."

Cara stood up and smiled at her gratefully. "Thanks Connie, I feel better already. I really didn't know who to talk to about this."

"You came to the right place. We RAs are here to help you solve your problems." Connie smiled. "I'll let you know what I've found out in a day or two, okay?"

"Great, thanks again." Cara waved good-bye as she left the room, hoping she and Ellis could get through another day or two without killing each other.

Chapter 3

"Cara ... hey, Cara, are you in there?" Rapid knocking accompanied Chrissy's exuberant voice, making Caroline grimace. It was a good thing Ellis had already left for the Rocky Mountain Club or she'd be sure to make some snide comment about Chrissy's country manners.

"Come in, Chrissy," Caroline called.

Chrissy threw open the door and burst inside. She quickly looked around the room. "Ellis isn't here?" she asked with barely suppressed excitement.

Caroline shook her head.

"Great!" Chrissy flopped down on Ellis's light blue bedspread and grinned at Caroline expectantly. "Guess what's new!"

Caroline shrugged her shoulders. "I don't know, what's new?"

"Try to guess . . . oh well, never mind, you'd never guess in a million years." Chrissy grinned happily. "First of all, I got a letter from William today."

"That's great, Chrissy." Caroline forced a smile to her face. She wanted to be happy for Chrissy, but thoughts of William Powell only brought to mind thoughts of Luke, and those were still so painful. "What did he have to say?"

Chrissy leaned forward eagerly. "He's so terrific, Cara. I mean, I just can't believe I'm so lucky! He said he had a great time here last weekend, and he misses me like crazy. Oh Cara, it's only been a week since I've seen him, but I miss him too."

"You really like him, don't you?" Caroline asked softly, noticing the pretty flush on her cousin's face and the brilliant sparkle of her blue eyes.

"Yeah, I do." Chrissy's flush deepened. "Oh, Cara, he's so nice, and we seem to have so much in common."

"I'm really happy for you, Chrissy," Caroline replied. "Just remember, long distance relationships seem to have a lot of pitfalls."

"I know, but we've talked about that and we decided it's definitely worth taking a chance. It's just something we have to deal with." She shrugged her shoulders. "*C'est la vie.*"

"At least your French is improving," Caroline grinned dryly.

"Anyway, that's not all my news." Chrissy jumped up from Ellis's bed and began pacing the floor in front of her cousin. "I had that meeting with Professor Pauly this afternoon and he wants me to write a column for the school newspaper." She stopped pacing and looked at Caroline proudly. "I'm going to be the official roving social reporter."

Caroline looked at her cousin dubiously. "A social reporter, what's that?"

"I'm supposed to report on all the social activities going on around the campus." Chrissy flopped back down on Ellis's bed, making Caroline cringe as she imagined the wrinkles her cousin was creating on the blue bedspread. "Professor Pauly told me to have fun with the column, to make it a column everyone will want to read each week."

"How are you going to do that?" Caroline asked curiously.

Chrissy shrugged with a sheepish grin. "I'm not sure, but I know I'll think of something."

Caroline looked at her with a touch of envy. *Why is Chrissy always so confident,* she thought. *Suddenly her life seems to be right on track. She's getting letters from a great guy who she's crazy about, and now she's been offered an exciting new challenge.* She sighed. *My life at the moment is the total pits.*

"What's wrong, Cara?" Chrissy asked sympathetically, making Cara realize that her unhappiness must have been reflected on her face. "Are you and Ellis still having problems?"

Caroline nodded with a deep sigh. "I talked to Connie earlier this evening, and she's going to see what she can do about getting me transferred to another room."

"Well, that's good news," Chrissy said brightly.

"I suppose," Caroline said hesitantly, pulling her knees up to her chest and leaning against the wall next to her bed. "I'm just feeling really confused lately about what I want. That fiasco with the Music Society has made me do a lot of thinking." She paused a moment and heaved another deep sigh. "It's funny, the things that used to be important to me don't seem to be so important anymore."

"Like what?" Chrissy asked.

Caroline shrugged helplessly, not sure if she could explain to Chrissy what she was feeling. "I don't know. All the things like belonging to the best clubs and knowing all the 'best' people don't mean much to me anymore. Even having French Literature as a major seems sort of silly now. I guess I'm just going through some sort of sophomore slump," she finished unhappily.

Chrissy grinned. "You can't be going through a sophomore slump, you're only a freshman."

"I've always been advanced for my age," Caroline answered without humor.

Chrissy jumped off of Ellis's bed. "What you need is to get out of this room and have a little fun. Come on, I'll treat you to a Coke at the Rocky Mountain Club."

"No, I'd rather not," Caroline said quickly.

"Come on, Cara. It'll be fun. There's always a bunch of kids there," Chrissy urged.

"But Ellis and her friends are there tonight," Caroline told her.

"So what?" Chrissy grabbed Caroline's hand and tugged her off the bed. "You're not going to let Ellis and her snobbish gossipy friends keep you from having a good time, are you?" Chrissy looked at her cousin defiantly.

"You're right," Caroline agreed with a small smile. "I can't spend my whole four years at C.U. avoiding Ellis and the Music Society."

Besides, Cara thought as she and Chrissy walked out of the room, *Ellis thinks Chrissy is gauche and provincial. She won't come within ten feet of me, if I'm with her!*

The Rocky Mountain Club was always noisy and crowded, and this evening was no different. The jukebox in the corner blared the latest Bruce Springsteen song, as if trying to override the chattering and laughing of the students who were packed into the room. As Chrissy and Caroline made their way through the throng of tables and kids to an empty booth, Chrissy yelled and waved to several of the students they passed. *She's so open and friendly,* Caroline thought enviously. *I wish it were as easy for me to make new friends.* The two cousins found an empty table and sat down, each ordering a Coke from the waitress who appeared at their table as if by magic.

"Hi, Cara; hi, Chrissy."

They turned and waved at the dark-haired, muscular guy sitting at a nearby table. "Hi Joe," they both answered, then grinned at each other. Joe Thornton had been the object of one of the cousins' first major college fights. Chrissy had met Joe when she had joined the Climbing Club, and by the end of the club's first camping trip, she had developed a mad crush on the handsome guy. Unfortunately, Joe had developed a mad crush on Cara.

"It looks like we've been abandoned," Caroline said, gesturing to the petite, blond-haired girl Joe was sitting with, his dark eyes gazing at her intently.

Chrissy grinned. "It's funny, two weeks ago, it would have bothered me to see Joe with somebody else, but since I met William, I don't care anymore."

"Have you ever noticed how the same kids almost always sit at the same tables," Caroline observed, looking around the room with interest. A small flush covered her face as she spotted Ellis and a couple of other members of the Music Society sitting at a corner table near the juke box.

"Yeah, I guess where you sit is sort of like a social statement," Chrissy exclaimed, her eyes widening as an idea began to form in her head. "Hey, that would make a great first column for me!" She thought for a moment. "All the shy kids always sit at the table nearest the front door. It's as if they're too shy to walk around and find another table."

"The few times that Ellis comes, she and her friends always sit at the table closest to the juke box," Cara added.

"That's the table for kids who aren't deep enough to carry on a real conversation, so they don't mind if the juke box drowns them out," Chrissy exclaimed, making Caroline giggle in appreciation. "And the nerds always sit at the food counter as if they can compensate for not having friends by eating!" Chrissy pulled a small notepad from her purse and began scribbling notes. "Oh, Cara, this is going to be great!"

Caroline watched her cousin writing notes with enthusiasm, and she felt an overwhelming loneliness. *Mon dieu, Chrissy is so excited about this column, and about William and about everything. She's so lucky to have things to be so enthusiastic about. What do I have? I hate my roommate and my classes are boring.* She stared glumly into her glass of Coke. *And what's worse, unless things change drastically, I have a feeling I'm going to hate the next four years of college life!*

Caroline knocked hesitantly on the door of room 212.

"Come in," a voice called through the door.

Caroline opened the door and practically

tripped over a pile of suitcases and boxes. "Hi, I'm Caroline Kirby. Connie told me I could start moving in some things this afternoon," she explained to the tall, dark-haired girl who was sitting on a suitcase, apparently trying to get it fastened.

"Hi, I'm Susan Whittier," she gave Caroline a friendly smile. "I'll be out of here in just a few minutes. This is my last suitcase."

"Would you like some help with that?" Caroline offered.

"I think I got it," she said just as the buckle clicked into place. "I can't believe how much junk I've accumulated while living in this room!"

"It must be exciting, getting married and starting a whole new life," Caroline said, feeling a pang touch her heart as she thought of Luke.

"Oh, it's not going to be too new of a life. Jonathon and I are only moving a block away from here, and we'll still be going to classes and being students." She gave Caroline a bright smile. "But, it will be wonderful to be married to him."

Caroline returned her smile, wondering if she would ever find the special somebody who would make her smile as radiantly as Susan was right now. Susan stood up and glanced out the window that overlooked the front of Fielding Hall. "Just in time. I see Jonathan pulling up out front." She turned and faced Cara with a happy grin. "Well, Caroline Kirby, good luck in your new room."

"Thanks, good luck with your marriage," Caroline told her sincerely. "Oh, what about those books on the desk?" she asked as her gaze fell on a stack of books that hadn't been packed.

"Oh darn," Susan huffed in exasperation. "I forgot all about those books. I used them for tutoring over at the prison. I was supposed to return them to the sociology department."

"I can return them for you," Caroline offered, picking up one of the books and thumbing through it with interest. "You tutored at a prison?"

Susan nodded, lifting the suitcase off the bed and onto the floor with the others. "It's part of a volunteer program sponsored by the sociology department. Anyone can participate. I went once a week to the prison to tutor inmates for their high school equivalency tests. If you think you might be interested, talk to Dr. Keenan in Sociology, she'll be able to give you all the details."

Caroline nodded as Susan raced out of the room to meet her fiancé. She placed the book back on the stack and walked around the room slowly. She'd been so happy that morning when Connie had told her the room transfer had been approved and she could move in this afternoon. Although the room was very small, she knew with her organizational skills the space would be more than adequate. Besides, there would be no more snide comments, no more snobbish retorts, no tension, no hassles. She'd be willing to live in a mousehole if it meant being able to move out of Ellis's room.

She walked back over to the desk and once again picked up one of the textbooks. *Tutoring prison inmates,* Caroline thought, *now that's a worthy cause. I bet I could do that.* It would be something entirely different than anything she had ever done in her life. The idea was intriguing.

"Maybe I've been too self-centered this last week," she said softly. "Maybe I'd feel better about myself if I helped someone else for a change, instead of dwelling on my own problems." It couldn't hurt to just talk to Dr. Keenan and find out the details.

Chapter 4

Caroline stood before the gates of the Colorado State Correctional Facility, her heart beating wildly in anticipation. Ever since she had spoken to Dr. Keenan the day before about volunteering, she'd been excited, but nervous, too.

At least I'm finally going to be doing something good and worthwhile, she decided, studying the sprawling gray one-story building before her. *It doesn't look anything like a prison,* she thought. With the uniform-sized windows and the drab, gray color, the building could have been a school, a hospital, or any institution.

Caroline clutched the textbooks against her for reassurance and walked purposefully up the large concrete walkway that led up to the double front door. Taking a deep breath, she pulled on one of the larger metal door handles, but the door didn't move. She tugged at the door again, harder, but with the same result. *What am I supposed to do now? Dr. Keenan told me they would be expecting me at two o'clock.* She looked down at her wristwatch. It was exactly two o'clock. She stepped back and eyed the locked, double doors. *Short of committing a crime, how am I supposed to get inside?*

"Please state your name and your business." Caroline squealed and jumped in surprise at the sound of the loud, booming voice that spoke from directly in front of her. It was then she saw the small camera above her, and a built-in speaker box next to the front doors. She leaned over and spoke into the speaker.

"Uh . . . my name is Caroline Kirby and I'm here to . . ."

"Please press the red button to speak," the authoritative voice interrupted her.

Caroline looked around in frustration, then spying the small, red button at the bottom of the speaker box, she pressed it and repeated her message. When she was finished, there was a loud buzz and she pulled open the door and stepped inside the prison.

Immediately, a woman in a light blue uniform approached her. "Caroline Kirby?"

Caroline nodded.

"Would you please come with me," the woman said, turning and leading Caroline into a small room. "You'll need to leave your purse and other personal belongings in here, and I'll need to see your books." She smiled apologetically. "Our building may not look like an official prison, but we still have to take certain precautionary measures." She took the books from Caroline, quickly thumbed through them, then handed them back to her. "You can pick up your personal belongings on your way out," she explained. "Now, if you'll just walk through here, I'll take you to your assigned inmate." She led Caroline through a metal detector, similar to the ones used at airports, then she motioned for Cara to follow her down another corridor.

"You've been assigned to tutor Sonny Maxwell," the matron explained as they walked down the corridor. "He's very bright, all he needs is some guidance and direction," she said as she motioned Caroline into a large room that looked like a huge recreation room. At one end there was a Ping-Pong table, and scattered about the rest of the room were tables and chairs. A television set was bolted into one wall, it's volume drowned out by the murmurings of other tutors working with inmates at several of the tables.

"If you'll just have a seat, Sonny will be brought out in just a few minutes."

Caroline nodded and sat down at one of the empty tables, looking around her with interest. *This is really quite pleasant,* she thought with a touch of relief. If it wasn't for the four uniformed guards that stood against each wall of the room, she could easily have imagined herself at a YMCA or a community center.

I wonder what Sonny Maxwell will be like, she thought, studying the inmates at the other tables. It was easy to distinguish the inmates from the volunteers. The inmates were all dressed alike in baggy, gray uniforms. *But they don't look like criminals,* she thought. They came in all shapes and sizes, but none of them had shifty eyes or mean faces like she'd expected. *They're just normal-looking, regular people. Sonny Maxwell could be middle-aged. He could look like a bank president or a grocery store clerk,* Caroline thought.

She looked up as a guard appeared in the doorway of the recreation room. Her eyes widened when she saw the inmate standing next to him. *He's so young,* she marveled. *He doesn't look much older than me!* She watched as he approached the table where she was sitting, stopping when he was standing directly in front of her.

"Hi, I'm Sonny Maxwell." He smiled fully at her.

Caroline felt her breath catch in her throat as she stared up at him. She certainly hadn't been expecting this—Sonny Maxwell was the most devastatingly handsome guy she had ever seen!

"Hi, I'm Caroline Kirby," she replied, feeling a light flush covering her face. He sat down in the chair opposite and the guard who had accompanied him drifted off to stand against the wall.

"Wow, if I'd known that the tutors looked like you, I would have decided to get my GED a long time ago!" he said, his bright blue eyes flirting with her, making her blush deepen.

This tutoring may be fun and exciting in more ways than one, Caroline thought to herself as she smiled at him shyly.

Chrissy grabbed a copy of the latest *Campus Times* from the rack in the Student Union and quickly thumbed through the pages.

"Wow!" she exclaimed as she turned to page four. There it was, her very first column!

"Holy mazoly!" She squealed in excitement. The editors had even given the column a name: Campus Chrissy. She squealed again. Holy cow, her name sure looked terrific in print!

"Hey, Chrissy! What's going on?"

Chrissy looked up from the paper to see Nan Sanderson approaching her. Chrissy and Nan had met one afternoon playing frisbee, and it had been Nan who had introduced Chrissy to the Climbing Club. The two girls had struck up an instant friendship.

"Nan . . . look at this!" Chrissy thrust the newspaper beneath Nan's nose.

"So what?" Nan replied after reading for a moment. "What's so exciting about three reported cases of measles at the school infirmary?"

"Not that," Chrissy scoffed in exasperation. "This article!" She pointed to her column.

As Nan read the article, Chrissy watched her friend's reactions closely, feeling a warm glow of pride as Nan began to laugh uproariously.

"Oh Chrissy, this is great!" Nan exclaimed, wiping tears of laughter from her brown eyes. "And it's all so true, everything you've said about where kids sit in the Rocky Mountain Club!" She giggled again. "I love this beginning part," she exclaimed and read aloud. " 'All of us have heard the old adage, you are what you eat, but no longer is what you eat important. The important thing today is *where* you eat, not *what* you eat!' " She handed the newspaper back to Chrissy with a look of admiration. "I didn't know you could write!"

Chrissy grinned sheepishly. "I wasn't sure either," she admitted, "but once I got the first couple of lines down on paper, the words just started to flow." She shook her head, grinning widely as she remembered how easily the column had transferred from an idea in her head to a humorous, tongue-in-cheek article. "I hope they all write as easy as this one. I'm supposed to write a column each week."

"I don't see how you're going to top this article!" Nan said, looking at Chrissy curiously. "What are you going to write about next?"

Chrissy shrugged, folding up the newspaper and placing it between the pages of her biology textbook. "I'm not sure, I've heard there's going to be a couple of club parties this weekend. I guess I'll attend them all, then decide which one

I'll write about in my column." She gave an expression of mock pain. "Professor Pauly made it clear that I'm to attend all the parties, banquets and dances on campus. It's a dirty job, but somebody has to do it!"

Nan grinned at her. "Sure, just let me know if you decide to resign and I'll take over your column. I wouldn't mind having a crack at a horrible job like that!"

Together the two girls laughed.

"Come on," Nan said with a grin. "I'll treat you to a Coke at the Rocky Mountain Club, sort of a celebration of your first column."

Chrissy looked at her wristwatch and nodded. "I've just got time for a quick Coke before my next class."

"Aren't you going to feel funny going to all the dances and parties by yourself?" Nan asked as the two of them moved toward the door that led downstairs to the Rocky Mountain Club.

"No, in fact, it's really perfect," Chrissy told her. "William and I have agreed not to date other people, so this way I can go to the parties and dances and have fun and I have a reason to go alone."

"I can see it now." Nan grinned. "You'll be the new Robin Leach, reporting on the life-styles of the rich and famous."

"Sure, only my column will be more on the life-styles of the young and restless." Chrissy giggled.

"Seriously, Chrissy. You should think of some sort of trademark for yourself," Nan exclaimed as they started down the stairs. "You know, like

Robin Leach has his affected voice and accent."

"Are you suggesting I try to talk with a proper English accent?" Chrissy laughed at the idea.

"Not necessarily, but if you're going to be an investigative reporter, you do need a trademark. That way everyone will know who you are by your trademark. Of course, if the column doesn't catch on with the kids, you don't have to worry about a trademark," Nan finished.

"Of course my column is going to catch on, it's going to be a big hit!" Chrissy paused thoughtfully at the entrance of the Rocky Mountain Club. "Maybe I should start wearing a scarf," she began thoughtfully. "No, not a scarf, because if somebody doesn't like one of my columns, they could strangle me with my trademark. What about a hat? I like the idea of wearing a hat!" she said thoughtfully, turning to Nan. "What do you think, should I find myself a hat to wear?"

Nan laughed and pulled her toward the café. "I think we should go in and get our Cokes before it's time for your next class. You're not quite Miss Social Column yet!"

Chrissy flashed Nan a grin, and together the two girls walked into the Rocky Mountain Club. They both stopped in their tracks just inside the door and stared around them speechlessly.

As usual, the Rocky Mountain Club was packed with students and the noise level was explosive. The center tables were overcrowded; with two and sometimes three people in each chair. Chrissy stared at the empty stools at the food counter, the stools where she had written only the nerds of the campus sat. Then she turned to the table nearest to the juke box; where she'd claimed the snobby kids usually sat. But no one was there today. Everyone had gathered smack in the middle of the club.

"You don't think this has anything to do with my column, do you?" Chrissy asked Nan with astonishment. "I mean, surely those empty stools and chairs are just some sort of wild coincidence." She looked at Nan with widened blue eyes. "I've heard of the power of the press, but you don't really believe my column did this . . . do you?"

Nan grinned widely. "I don't know, Chrissy. But I think it's time you find yourself a hat!"

Chapter 5

"Hey, Cara . . . wait up!"

Caroline paused on the library steps, watching as Chrissy raced across the browning grass that separated Butler Library from the Student Union. *She looks like a wild ten-year-old kid,* Caroline thought with a smile, watching as Chrissy hurdled a small hedge, her blond hair flying in all directions. Chrissy skidded to a halt in front of her.

"Where have you been?" Chrissy demanded. "I looked all over for you yesterday afternoon, but I couldn't find you anywhere!"

"I was in prison yesterday," Caroline replied with a mysterious smile.

"In prison?" Chrissy stared at Caroline with widened eyes. "What prison? What for? Cara, are you in some kind of trouble?" Chrissy looked at her cousin worriedly.

"No, I'm not in any kind of trouble," she assured Chrissy with a small smile. "In fact, I feel like I'm finally doing something right with my life!"

"Caroline Kirby, I don't know what's going on, but I think it's time we had a cousin-to-cousin talk!" Chrissy exclaimed, grabbing Caroline's arm and pulling her to a nearby bench. Once they were both seated, Chrissy looked at Caroline expectantly. "Now, tell me what right thing you're doing at a prison!" she demanded.

"You know Susan Whittier, the girl whose room I took? Well, on the day she was moving out and I was moving in, she told me about this volunteer program through the sociology department. I'm tutoring an inmate for his high school equivalency test."

Chrissy looked at her cousin in horror. "Tutoring an inmate—you mean like a criminal?" Chrissy's voice registered her shock. "Cara, that sounds really dangerous."

"*Mon dieu*, Chrissy." Caroline laughed softly. "You make it sound like I'm going into a dark alley with Jack the Ripper!" she scoffed. "There's nothing dangerous about it. The tutoring takes place in a large recreation room. Yesterday was my first time and I really think I'm going to like it."

Chrissy looked at her cousin dubiously. It didn't seem possible that Caroline, the girl who loved the ballet and the opera, the girl who wanted to know the 'best' people and belong to the most exclusive clubs, was actually going to enjoy tutoring inmates at a prison! Still, Chrissy had to admit, Caroline was showing the first spark of life since they had come back from their visit to Fort Collins. Maybe this would take her mind off her breakup with Luke.

"So, who are you tutoring?" Chrissy asked curiously.

"A guy named Sonny Maxwell." Caroline leaned toward Chrissy eagerly. "Oh, Chrissy, you should see this guy, he's got the most gorgeous blond hair and blue eyes. He's twenty-four years old, and really nice!" A light flush reddened Caroline's cheeks as she remembered how flirtatious Sonny had been the day before.

"Holy mazoly, Cara, you sound like you're hung up on the guy!" Chrissy exclaimed.

"Don't be ridiculous," Caroline retorted defensively. "I'm not like you. I don't fall head over heels in love with every good-looking guy who says hello to me."

Chrissy flushed. "I don't do that," she said tightly, knowing Caroline was referring to Joe Thornton. Chrissy couldn't help it that she had mistaken Joe's natural friendliness for romantic interest!

"You right, I'm sorry," Caroline said with a light blush. "It's just that I don't want you to think I'd be crazy enough to fall for a guy who's in prison. Honestly, Chrissy, give me a little credit!"

"Okay, so what's he in prison for?" Chrissy asked.

Caroline looked at Chrissy in surprise. "I don't know. We didn't get around to talking about anything really personal yesterday. We mostly just worked." She paused for a moment, remembering how difficult it had been for her to concentrate on working when Sonny kept grinning at her, his blue eyes dancing attractively. "He seems to be really smart," she added thoughtfully.

"He can't be too smart if he's in prison," Chrissy said dryly.

"You know what I mean," Caroline returned impatiently. "Anyway, I'm finally doing something good and worthwhile. If Sonny can get his high school equivalency, then when he gets out of prison he can get a good job and lead a crime-free life."

Chrissy thought of all sorts of reasons why she didn't think it was a good idea for Caroline to be working in a prison. *I don't care what Cara says, it sounds dangerous to me. And I sure don't like the way Caroline looked just then when she was talking about this Sonny Maxwell.* But as Chrissy looked at Cara's face lit with animation, she decided not to say anything. Besides, they were both in college now, and that meant they were old enough to make their own choices.

"Well . . . if this is what you want to do . . ." Chrissy said, her voice reflecting her doubts.

"Oh, it is!" Caroline assured her. "Now, enough

about what I'm doing. Why were you looking all over for me yesterday?"

Chrissy's face lit up as she fumbled in her books. She pulled out a creased, well-read copy of the latest *Campus Times* and handed it to Cara.

"Your column came out!" Caroline smiled, scanning the column quickly. "That's really nice," she said when she was finished.

"Nice! It's better than nice, it's great! You should hear all the kids talking about it," Chrissy snatched back the newspaper, irritated by Caroline's lack of enthusiasm for her column.

"Look, Chrissy, I've got to run." Caroline stood up from the bench. "I've got to work out some lesson plans for Sonny, and I've got tons of homework from my classes. They may be boring, but I've still got to keep up with the work."

"Yeah, okay." Chrissy stood up, her bright smile of a few minutes ago gone.

"Chrissy, your column was really very good," Caroline said, pleased when Chrissy flashed her a happy smile. "I'll see you later." She waved good-bye to Chrissy, then began walking across the campus toward her dormitory.

It was difficult for her to be enthusiastic about Chrissy's article. The whole column had seemed so shallow! Couldn't Chrissy have found something more important to write about than where people sat to eat in the Rocky Mountain Club? *There are so many more important things in life than the social ramifications of where kids sit to eat. Important things like helping men put their*

*lives back together and giving them the tools to
lead full, useful lives,* she thought. She picked up
her pace, not even noticing the November chill in
the air.

When Chrissy had stopped her, she'd been in
the library checking out some remedial math and
reading books. While working with Sonny yesterday she'd noticed he was sadly lacking in basic
math skills and his reading was atrocious. But he
was bright, and he had absorbed what little she'd
taught him like a sponge, and she was anxious to
bring him up to his full potential. *Maybe the people at the prison will let me work with Sonny
every day instead of only three days a week,* she
thought. *Then we could really make great progress.* Besides, she'd found working with Sonny an
almost exhilarating experience. He was so bright
and witty and he'd looked at her in a way that
had made her feel sort of shy and breathless.

She scoffed at these thoughts. She was being
silly. She'd felt exhilarated because she was
happy to be doing something worthwhile instead
of worrying about such superficial things as what
clothes to wear and what club to join. It had nothing whatsoever to do with the fact that Sonny
was an extremely handsome guy!

She lifted her large stack of books from one hip
to the other. She would have to read all the books
she'd checked out to see which ones would be the
most useful. She'd probably be up all night. She
smiled happily to herself. It was so nice to finally
have a worthwhile goal!

* * *

"What do you think!" Chrissy turned and looked at Denise, the wide-brimmed straw hat sitting squarely on top of her head.

Denise looked at her critically. "No. That one makes you look like a scarecrow in a cornfield." She picked up a small, wool beret. "Try this one."

The two girls had taken a bus from campus to the downtown Boulder Mall, and for the past half hour they had been shopping in the Hat Rack Boutique.

Chrissy frowned at her reflection. "No, this won't work, either," she said, eyeing the royal blue beret with disgust. "Maybe I should just forget the hat and go with something else as a trademark."

"No, Nan was right, a hat would be perfect," Denise replied. "What about this one." She picked up a beige fedora and plopped it on Chrissy's head.

Chrissy studied her reflection thoughtfully. "All I need is a trenchcoat and I'd look like James Bond," she said with a grin. She turned and modeled the hat for Denise. "What do you think?"

"It's perfect!" Denise proclaimed with a small giggle. "It makes you look sort of mysterious and romantic."

"Sold!" Chrissy laughed. She definitely liked the idea of being a mysterious, romantic reporter.

"Why don't we get a frozen yogurt and relax before we catch a bus back to campus," Denise suggested as Chrissy paid for her hat.

"Sounds good," Chrissy agreed. She took her change and walked with Denise outside into the streets where people were strolling in and out of the boutiques, galleries, and restaurants that lined the way.

The girls paused a moment to watch a mime performing for a small crowd of people who had gathered around him. They laughed in delight as the mime pretended he was in an invisible box. The girls continued on, bought some frozen yogurt, then found a park bench where they sat and ate their yogurt and people-watched.

"Wow, look at those two hunks," Denise whispered as two attractive young men walked by. "But I suppose since William called you last night, you don't even want to look at other guys."

Chrissy giggled. "Denise, I may be crazy about William, but I'm not blind, and I haven't lost my appreciation for the finer things in life!" Chrissy scooped a spoonful of yogurt into her mouth, thinking happily of William's phone call the night before. They had talked for nearly an hour, and it had been so wonderful to hear his voice again. They'd talked about everything and nothing, but just hearing his voice had made Chrissy realize how much she really did care about him.

"So, what's your next column going to be about!" Denise asked.

"I'm not sure. I'm thinking about writing one on the uselessness of some of the clubs around campus." She looked at Denise incredulously.

"Did you know there's a chocolate-lovers club on campus?"

"Hmmm, that's a club I should join," Denise exclaimed, spooning some of her chocolate yogurt into her mouth with a grin.

"I'm serious!" Chrissy said. "They have clubs for the underweight, the overweight, the depressed and the hyper. I'm surprised they don't have a club for students who have more than one pimple!"

"But that would be nearly everyone on campus at one time or another," Denise said giggling.

"I figure this week I'll write an article about clubs in general," Chrissy went on. "Then I'll end the column by saying that I'm going to be reporting on various club activities in the future. That way, the clubs who want me to report on them will invite me to all their functions."

"Sounds like a great scam to improve your social life," Denise teased.

"Denise, how can you even suggest such a thing!" Chrissy looked at her roommate with mock outrage. "This is strictly a job. How can you even think I'm going to enjoy going to all the dances, eating all that banquet food, and reporting all the gossip I hear."

"Yeah," Denise replied dryly. "It sounds like a real nightmare."

"More like a terrific dream," Chrissy said, wiggling her eyebrows in a Gracho Marx imitation.

The two girls looked at each other and broke out into gales of laughter.

Chapter 6

"Nice sweater," Sonny commented, his dark blue eyes gazing at the peach-colored sweater Caroline was wearing.

"Thanks." Caroline blushed lightly. She and Sonny had just completed the lesson she had worked up for today, and there was still a few minutes left before the session time was up.

"You look pretty in pastels and soft colors," Sonny said. "But, a girl as pretty as you would look good in almost everything."

"Thank you," Caroline said again, feeling her blush deepen. She glanced away in embarrassment, but still could sense his unwavering gaze. *I shouldn't be feeling like this,* she reminded herself. *I'm supposed to be tutoring Sonny, not flirting with him.*

"I'll bet the cost of a sweater like that would have fed my brothers and sisters for a week," Sonny observed softly.

"How many brothers and sisters do you have?" Caroline asked.

In the past week of tutoring Sonny, there had been very little personal conversation between them. Although Caroline had found herself attracted to Sonny, she had so far managed to keep their conversations strictly on the business of tutoring. Reading and math had been the main subjects of discussion, but now Caroline's curiosity got the better of her.

"Four brothers and two sisters. I'm the oldest." Sonny paused a moment and shook his head sadly. "They're part of the reason I'm here."

Caroline leaned toward him intrigued to learn more about the handsome young man. He was so attractive and so charming, and he seemed like such a nice guy, that Caroline had been wondering since the day she'd met Sonny what circumstances had brought him to prison. She couldn't imagine him doing anything bad or illegal.

"How are your brothers and sisters part of the reason you're in here?" she asked.

"My old man left my mother when my youngest sister was born. He just disappeared one day and we never heard from him again. That left my Mom with seven of us to clothe and feed." Sonny's voice held a touch of bitterness. "I had to quit school when I was thirteen to go to work and help put food on the table."

"Thirteen," Caroline echoed in amazement. "What sort of work did you do?" She tried to imagine having to go to work at such a young age. *Mama mia, when I was thirteen, my world consisted of ballet lessons and family vacations to Europe. The biggest problem I ever faced was what to wear to school.* Caroline ventured a smile at the young man opposite. Poor Sonny.

"I lied about my age and worked all sorts of jobs," Sonny answered. "I swept floors and cleaned up garbage, whatever else I could find that would pay me something." He smiled sheepishly. "I was seventeen when I made by first mistake. I robbed my first house and discovered I could make more in a single night than I could make in a full week at a regular job. That was the beginning of the end."

"Didn't you ever think about getting caught?" Caroline asked.

"Sure, it crossed my mind, but when my brothers and sisters were crying from hunger, or when they didn't have coats to wear in the winter, the consequences of my actions sort of slipped my mind." He gave her another sheepish smile. "At the time I didn't think there were any other alternatives."

"It doesn't seem quite fair, does it?" Caroline asked reflectively. "I mean, some people have so much, and other people have so little." She felt a tinge of guilt as she realized she was one of the people who'd always had so much. She had loving, supportive parents and she'd never in her life had to worry about where her next meal was coming from. It somehow made her feel slightly ashamed.

"Yeah, I guess life deals out a pretty crummy hand to some people," Sonny agreed. "But that's all behind me now." Sonny flashed her a confident smile. "With a high school equivalency behind me, I can get a good job when I get out of here in two years."

"Maybe after you get your high school diploma, you could take a couple of correspondence college courses," Caroline suggested. "A little bit of a college background would really improve your job prospects." She looked at him curiously. "Have you thought about what sort of work you'd like to do when you get out?"

"I'm really not sure, I haven't given it much thought. I just know what sort of work I won't ever do again! You know, I like the idea of taking some college classes. That's a great idea," Sonny exclaimed, his blue eyes soft with gratitude. "I really appreciate all the help you're giving me, Caroline. You don't know how much I look forward to your coming here." Caroline felt her heart do a little flip-flop in her chest at his words. He looked down at the table, his expression suddenly sad. "You're the only visitor I ever get."

"But what about your family?" Caroline asked in astonishment.

Sonny shook his head. "My family lives in Denver, and it's not easy for my mom to come out to Boulder without a car. Besides it's impossible for her to get away from the kids and come and visit. And anyway," his face flushed darkly, "I wouldn't want any of them to see me in here."

"But what about friends?" Caroline pressed.

Sonny shrugged, once again a tinge of bitterness in his eyes. "You don't make many friends in the business I was in. I do have one good friend who lives not far away, but he hasn't come to see me since I've been here."

Caroline's heart expanded in sympathy. She couldn't imagine being so alone in the world. Oh, how unfair life was for Sonny. "I could ask to see if I could come more often," she suggested shyly, hurriedly adding, "We'd be able to get a lot of work done if I could come and see you every day."

"Oh wow, that would be great!" Sonny's face lit up. "Caroline Kirby, you are the greatest thing that's ever happened to me. With your help, I'm really going to turn my life around!"

Caroline's heart expanded happily at Sonny's words. It was so great to be needed, and it was especially wonderful to be needed by a guy like Sonny!

Fifteen minutes later when Caroline left the prison, she was still glowing from Sonny's words. It was a new feeling for her, to feel the pride of accomplishing something so worthwhile for somebody else. *And now I'll be seeing Sonny every day*, she thought. *I'm glad the matron agreed that Sonny would progress quicker if I came more often.*

"I've got to get a bicycle," she said aloud, dreading the thirty minute walk back to the campus. Lots of people used bicycles to get around Boulder, and a bicycle would cut her walking time in half. Suddenly she jumped as the bushes next to her rustled loudly. She stepped backward and stared at the large bush. Had one of the prisoners escaped? Were they hiding in the bush ready to make good on an escape?

A giggle bubbled to her lips as the 'escaping convict' showed himself with a plaintive meow.

"Hello, kitty." She leaned down and petted the black cat that curled itself around her legs. "You're so skinny," she murmured, gently scratching the cat's thin sides. The cat lifted its head and looked at her, revealing a pretty white face and large green eyes. "Go home, kitty," she said, giving the cat a final scratch and straightening up. She began to walk away, surprised when the cat stayed right at her heels. She turned back to the cat. "Go on, go home!" The cat sat down and looked up at her, then meowed again. "What's the matter, don't you have a home?" The cat walked over and rubbed its back against Cara's leg. "You look so hungry," Cara murmured, picking up the cat and scratching it behind its ears. "I'll see if I can't find you something to eat. But once I feed you, you're on your own," she warned, snuggling the cat against her chest. As she started her long walk back to the campus, the cat closed its eyes and purred loudly.

* * *

Chrissy stood behind a large, potted palm tree, her beige fedora pulled down low on her forehead. She'd wanted to view the Political Science Club meeting from a vantage point where she could see everything, but nobody could see her, and this tall plant in the corner of the conference room had been the perfect place.

She looked down at the small, black notebook in her hand and frowned. She'd been at the meeting for almost an hour and she had yet to write a single word.

"I could have gone to a Chess Club meeting, but I thought it would be boring. Hah! it probably would have been fascinating compared to the Political Science Club," she muttered with disgust to one of the large palm fronds that shielded her from view. This is boring, boring boring!"

Since her second column had appeared in the *Campus Times* two days earlier, Chrissy had been inundated with invitations to all kinds of events. It seemed that every club on the campus wanted the official thumbs-up from Chrissy, and were willing to take the risk of a possible thumbs-down.

She leaned forward eagerly as two of the Political Science Club members moved away from the group and near her palm tree. *Finally,* she thought. *Maybe now I'll hear some juicy club gossip.* She leaned forward a little bit more, straining to hear what the two young men were saying to each other.

"It's all set up for next Saturday morning at

nine o'clock. The Women's Forum is holding a demonstration in front of the library. We've got twelve guys showing up to heckle them," one bespectacled student whispered to the other.

"We've got to make sure that we can make enough of a ruckus that the Women's Forum won't be able to gain support," the other student replied.

Wow, this is great stuff! Chrissy thought with excitement. *They're planning on sabotaging a demonstration by the Women's Forum.* She grabbed her pen from her purse and quickly scribbled down the pertinent information, wondering exactly what sort of demonstration the Women's Forum was planning for Saturday morning. This was definitely news! Finally, her patience had paid off. She'd spent the past hour eavesdropping on half a dozen conversations and had been disappointed not to hear a single drop of good gossip. In fact, the only unusual thing she'd noticed about the Political Science Club was that the members were all guys. Until now, she'd thought they were actually discussing government policies. Now, finally, she had something great for her next column.

She dropped her pen and the notebook into her purse. *I've seen enough,* she thought. *Besides, it's late and I'm thirsty and tired of lurking behind this palm tree.* She looked longingly at the cups of punch set out on the refreshment table.

As she started to wriggle out from behind the potted plant, Chrissy tripped, accidentally stepping into the pot that held the huge palm plant. *Rats!* she cursed, feeling her foot sinking into the gushy mulch and soil. *Wouldn't you know they just watered the stupid thing,* she thought, attempting to pull her foot out of the mess. She tugged, but her foot didn't move. She pulled a little harder, but still her foot wouldn't budge. Somehow, her foot had become wedged in the small space between the pot and the plant itself.

This is ridiculous, she scoffed. *Investigative reporters are supposed to hide behind plants, but they're not supposed to get stuck in them! Don't panic,* she instructed herself rationally. *Your foot went in, so it's got to come out!* She wiggled her foot, trying to work it out, but the foot remained firmly stuck.

What am I going to do? Chrissy wondered, *I'll have to stay here until the meeting finishes, and then if I can't get this stupid plant off, I'll have to walk back to my dorm room dragging it along with me. And then Denise will have to call the fire department to come and help me! I'll be in the newspaper, all right, but not as Campus Chrissy— more like Campus Klutz!*

In a last-ditch effort, she grabbed the plant around its broad base and tugged with all her might. "Ohhhhh," she squealed, feeling the heavy plant beginning to tip ominously to one side. "Ohhhh nooooo!" She groaned as both she and the plant tipped over and tumbled to the floor.

They hit the floor with a loud crash. For a

moment, Chrissy lay there in shock. Then she realized that in the fall, her foot had come unstuck! Slowly she sat up and brushed the potting soil off her skirt and blouse, her own eyes widening as she met a dozen pairs of eyes staring at her in surprise.

"Hi," Chrissy exclaimed to the stunned onlookers. "I'm Chrissy from The *Campus Times*. Could I get a cup of punch?" She smiled brightly.

The two guys who had been plotting to sabotage the demonstration on Saturday looked at each other, then advanced on Chrissy.

"Hey, wait a minute!" she objected as one of them grabbed her notebook and the other grabbed her by the arms. "Hey, you can't do that!" she yelled as the guy with the glasses tore a page out of her notebook and the other dragged her toward the door of the conference room.

"We don't need any snoops at our meetings!" he exclaimed, setting her on the concrete sidewalk outside.

"I'm not a snoop, I'm an investigative reporter!" Chrissy protested heatedly. She glared at the door to the conference room as it shut in her face. "You can't do this to me! I'm Campus Chrissy!" she yelled, grinning as the door opened again. *Ah ha, they've had second thoughts,* she thought triumphantly. *They're going to apologize. They know about the power of the press.*

But her smile turned to a grimace of frustration as her notebook came sailing out the open door and skidded on the concrete, landing at her feet.

Chapter 7

Chrissy yanked her coat up around her neck, walking briskly toward her dorm room in Culver Hall. *How dare they!* she seethed angrily, thinking about how she was treated by members of the Political Science Club. *How dare they treat me like I'm a piece of unwanted garbage, throwing me out on the sidewalk! They'll be sorry,* she thought, anticipating the scathing article that would appear in her next column. *I'll make sure they're sorry, and I'll also make sure and contact the Women's Forum and tell them about the Political Science Club's plans!*

"Chrissy . . . wait up!"

Chrissy turned and beneath the lights lining the sidewalk, she saw Nan hurrying toward her. "Hi

63

Nan, where are you going so late in the evening?" she asked curiously.

"I'm not going, I'm coming back from the library," Nan said as she caught up with Chrissy. "I was putting in some extra study time. You do remember we have a biology test tomorrow . . ."

"Oh jeez, I forgot all about the test!" Chrissy moaned, she'd have several hours studying ahead of her if she wanted to pass that biology test.

"Where have you been?" Nan asked, as the girls fell into step together.

"I was covering a Political Science Club meeting," Chrissy explained with a frown. "What a bunch of creeps!"

"What do you mean?" Nan laughed. "I always thought the Political Science Club members were pretty boring."

"Ha! They were boring until I discovered their plan to ruin a demonstration the Women's Forum has planned for this Saturday morning, then they threw me out of their meeting!" Chrissy fumed. "Imagine, me, Campus Chrissy, thrown out on the sidewalk!"

"I see," Nan said. "You mean the Poli-Sci Club didn't give you the respect you so richly deserve as an investigative reporter?"

"You can say that again! Those guys are going to have to learn that Campus Chrissy is not somebody to mess with!" she vowed, a mischievous gleam in her eye.

"Someone had better warn the Poli-Sci Club," Nan teased.

Chrissy gave her friend a look of mock indignation, then grinned. "Well, the good thing is I've discovered a great way to conduct my investigations of a club."

"What's that?" Nan asked, shivering slightly as a cold breeze suddenly whipped around them.

"From now on I'm going to work completely undercover, lurking behind bushes, peeking around corners, observing without anyone knowing I'm there," Chrissy explained. "That's how I found out about the Political Science Club's plans to sabotage the Women's Forum."

"So you'll be like Agent Double-Oh Seven?" Nan asked, her voice revealing more than a hint of skepticism.

"More like a Double-Oh Six," Chrissy confessed with a grin. "I'm not very good at staying hidden yet." She sobered slightly. "But that way I get a good idea of what the club is really like without anyone acting differently because they know Campus Chrissy is there."

"Sounds like a winning idea to me," Nan agreed, then shivered once again. "I've got to go in, I'm freezing!"

"Okay, I'll see you tomorrow in biology."

As Chrissy waved to her friend, a cloud of gloom descended over her at the thought of the biology test. *It's a good thing Nan reminded me, although I'll be up all night studying for that stupid test.* She shrugged. *I guess this is what college is all about—having fun, meeting new friends and staying up all night cramming for tests. It'd be perfect if I could just skip all those darned tests!*

She'd almost arrived at her own dorm when she decided on impulse to stop in at Fielding Hall and see Caroline for a few minutes.

It won't hurt to stop in and say hello, Chrissy thought, as usual finding it easy to put studying on a back burner in exchange for a social visit. *Besides, I've hardly seen Caroline for the last couple of days and I can tell her all about finding out the Poly Sci Club's plans to ruin the Women's Forum demonstration.*

Chrissy walked up the steps of Fielding Hall, thinking how she and Caroline had begun to drift apart since the beginning of college, and especially during the past few weeks. *Of course, part of the problem is that we have different classes and different interests,* Chrissy rationalized as she entered her cousin's dormitory. *It would have been easier if we could have been roommates, but c'est la vie. Still, Cara is not just my cousin, but also one of my very best friends in the whole wide world. Staying close to Cara is important—a lot more important than some stupid old biology test!* With this thought in mind, Chrissy raced down the hall toward Caroline's new room.

Caroline sat on the edge of her bed, the black cat curled up in her lap and filling the otherwise silent room with its contented purring.

"What am I going to do with you," she asked

the furry little creature. "I don't know what possessed me to smuggle you in here." But deep inside, Caroline knew why she had brought the cat into her room. She was lonely. She had thought it would be great to have a room all to herself, but she hadn't realized how lonely it would be. She smiled as the cat nuzzled her hand in an effort to get her to pet him. "You could get me into a lot of trouble," she said to the cat. "It's against dorm rules to have any animals in here." The cat meowed and rubbed the back of his head against her hand. "Okay, okay." Caroline laughed and scratched the cat behind his ears. "I'll let you stay for tonight. It's too cold for you to be outside wandering around." Caroline froze as somebody knocked on her door.

Who could that be this late at night? I hope nobody saw me bring the cat in here. Mon dieu, if anyone finds the cat in here, I'll really get into a lot of trouble, Caroline thought, frantically looking for a place to hide the cat.

"Uh . . . just a minute . . ." she called as the knocking resumed on the door.

"Cara, it's me; Chrissy. Open up!"

Caroline thought about sticking the cat in one of her dresser drawers, but instantly rejected the idea. The sharp little claws would tear her clothes to pieces. She dismissed putting the cat in the closet for the same reason.

Finally she shoved the cat under the bed, sighing with relief as the cat curled up in a little ball and closed his eyes. *Good, now I'll just get rid of*

Chrissy as quickly as possible. Caroline hurried over and opened the door.

"What took you so long?" Chrissy complained, walking into the room and looking at Caroline curiously.

"What do you want, Chrissy? I'm sort of busy," Caroline said, praying silently that the cat would take a nice long nap under the bed.

"You're always busy at the prison and I'm always busy with my column, and we never seem to see each other anymore," Chrissy explained, flopping down on the bed and making the bedsprings squeak noisily.

"We see each other almost every day around the campus," Caroline replied, hoping the cat didn't suddenly dart out from beneath the bed. While she knew that Chrissy would never intentionally get her in trouble, secrets always had a way of getting away from her, no matter how she tried to keep them to herself!

"I know we see each other every day, but we never seem to have any time to talk anymore," Chrissy complained, swinging her feet up and down on the side of the bed. "So, I decided to stop in for a little friendly conversation."

"This really·isn't a very good time." Caroline's voice slid an octave higher than usual as she saw two black paws and a little white nose appear just beneath the edge of the bedspread directly beneath Chrissy's swinging feet. "I've got tons of homework to do tonight, and I'm seeing Sonny every day now at the prison so I'm always busy with lesson plans. Plus I've got an art history paper due tomorrow and I haven't even started reading my research material and . . ."

"Cara, you're babbling," Chrissy giggled, looking at her cousin in astonishment.

"Well, of course I'm babbling." Caroline flushed as she noticed the cat's head sticking out from beneath the bed. He was eyeing Chrissy's swinging shoes as if they were some sort of delightful, teasing toys to pounce upon. "You come bursting into my room at ten o'clock at night when I have loads of work to do. You flop down on my bed without caring about wrinkling the spread." Caroline began to pace, hoping to distract the cat from Chrissy's swinging shoes.

"Well, excuse me!" Chrissy jumped up off the bed and stood up, the suddenness of her movements causing the cat to disappear back under the bed. "I didn't realize a visit from me was such an imposition!" she said stiffly, stung by her cousin's unfriendly attitude. She stalked regally past Caroline to the door. "When you decide it's convenient for me to visit you, just let me know!"

But before she could get out the door, Caroline grabbed her by the coat sleeve. "Chrissy, I'm sorry. You're right, that was very rude of me and I apologize," Caroline said earnestly. Now that Chrissy was halfway out the door, her secret was safe for the moment. "I've just really been bogged down with work since I started tutoring at the prison," she explained.

"That's okay," Chrissy replied, instantly forgiving. She knew better than anyone how uptight Caroline could get when she felt overwhelmed by work. "Anyway, I've got a big biology test tomorrow I need to study for, so I guess I'd better start studying."

"I'll tell you what," Caroline suggested. "Why don't we meet at the Rocky Mountain Club tomorrow, at about four o'clock? We can have a Coke and catch up with what's been going on for the last couple of days.

"That sounds great!" Chrissy smiled cheerfully. "I'll see you tomorrow at four!"

The minute Chrissy stepped out of the room, Caroline closed her door and leaned back against it with a sigh of relief.

"*Mama mia*, that was a close call!" She looked sternly at the cat, who was once again peeking out from beneath the edge of the bedspread. "If you aren't careful, you're really going to get me into trouble!"

The cat meowed.

"Trouble," Caroline said softly with a smile. "That's a perfect name for you." She walked over and picked up the cat. "We're going to have to get a box or something where we can hide you when someone comes in," she said, realizing that at some point she had come to the decision to keep the cat. She laughed as the cat licked her chin. "I think I'm going to like having you for a roommate, much better than that catty Ellis." Chuckling at her own pun, she snuggled the cat closer to her heart.

Chapter 8

"Come on, Caroline, tell me the truth, there must be a hundred of those college guys lined up to take you out every weekend," Sonny teased, his blue eyes sparkling at Caroline.

"No. Really, there's nobody," Caroline answered with a shy little laugh. "Actually, there was somebody special for a while, but we broke up a few weeks ago."

"Oh, I'm sorry." Sonny reached over to touch Caroline's hand sympathetically, but she jerked it back as if she had been burned by fire. Every day she spent with Sonny, she found herself more and more attracted to him. She knew it wasn't right, but she didn't know how to stop it.

"Actually, our breakup was probably for the best," she explained quickly, her gaze not quite meeting his. His eyes were so beautiful, she found it difficult to concentrate when she looked into them. "Sometimes I wish I could go back in time and change things," she said reflectively, thinking about the way Luke had found Robert's letter. "But I guess it was meant to be this way. Kind of like fate, you know?"

"Fate." Sonny said the word like it left a bitter taste in his mouth. "If breaking up with your boyfriend is the worst thing fate's handed you, then you've been lucky." He gestured around the prison recreation room. "Look where fate has gotten me." Caroline was silent under his penetrating gaze. She couldn't help that she'd been lucky.

"Even our values are totally different," Sonny went on.

"Just because our fates have been different doesn't mean our values have to be different," Caroline said.

"Caroline." Sonny smiled at her patiently, a soft smile that made Caroline's heart flutter. "The things that you have taken for granted all your life are the very things I value most—food, heat in the winter, clothing, electricity. We lived for two months with no electricity one summer, and I'll bet you grew up with air-conditioning and all the electrical appliances money could buy."

Caroline's face flushed guiltily as she thought of all the times she had left her electric curlers on, or had gone out for the day with her stereo playing.

"Don't look so shocked." Sonny laughed at her expression, but his laughter was kind. "It's obvious just by looking at you that one of your biggest values is physical appearance. Your clothes, your makeup, even your hairstyle . . . everything about you tells me that your parents raised you emphasizing the value of appearances."

"That's not true," Caroline replied, running a hand over her blond hair self-consciously. She flushed again. "Well, maybe it's sort of true," she admitted. *Sonny's right,* she thought. *I've grown up in such a privileged household, with never a thought for those who have less than me.* She looked at Sonny painfully. "Looking back, I feel like I've spent my entire life in some sort of worthless vacuum."

Sonny smiled in understanding. "It's not too late to change all that. You're already made a lot of progress just by questioning the values and ideals you were raised with. You've also made a positive step in volunteering your time in helping others here."

Caroline nodded slowly, thinking there was so much more she could be doing. In fact, she would talk to Dr. Keenan as soon as possible about tutoring another inmate or two. It was suddenly important to Caroline that she redeem herself and make up for her spoiled self-indulgent life. She wanted Sonny to know that she was changing, focusing on the real issues in life, not the superficial ones. *I want my life to really count for something,* she decided. *I can work the tutoring*

of a couple more inmates around my class sched-
ule, and if my grades slip a little bit, it really
doesn't matter. She sighed in disgust at herself.
I'm taking a bunch of silly, frivolous classes any-
way.

"Caroline . . ." Sonny looked at her hesitantly.
"I have a really big favor to ask you."

"What?" She smiled at him shyly. "You know
I'll do anything I can to help you."

"This is sort of a major favor," Sonny continued, lowering his voice to a mere whisper.
"Remember that friend I told you about, the one
who doesn't live too far from here?"

"The one who never comes to visit you?"
Caroline asked.

Sonny nodded. "Would you take him a note for
me?" Sonny looked around and Caroline knew he
was making sure that no one was watching as he
pulled a small, folded note from the pocket of his
uniform. He palmed the note and extended his
hand casually across the table to her.

"Sonny, I can't do that," Caroline answered in
a hushed whisper. She remembered only too well
all the warnings she had received from Dr.
Keenan about just this sort of thing. "Please,
Sonny, you know I'm not supposed to do that."

Sonny leaned closer to her across the table, his
blue eyes pleading with her. "Please, Caroline.
What's the harm? It's just a note asking Jake to
come and see me." Sonny looked at her humbly,
his voice still a low whisper. "Caroline, I'm beg-
ging you, please do this for me. Jake and I were

such close friends. He was like a brother to me, and I really miss seeing him. I know he'll come if he knows how much I want to see him. Please, Caroline!" He reached out his hand with the note in the palm and grabbed one of her hands. When he withdrew his hand, the note was in Caroline's palm. She quickly closed her hand to hide the note. "Jake's address is printed on the front of the note," he whispered.

"Okay," Caroline relented softly. How could she deny him this small request, especially when he was looking at her like she was the most wonderful thing in the world. "Just this once," she added, reminding herself again that no matter how handsome Sonny was, her job was to tutor him, and that was all.

"Thanks, Caroline." Sonny's eyes glittered brightly. "You will never know how thankful I am, and how much you've done for me!"

What's the harm? Caroline asked herself later as she walked back to the dorms from the prison. *It won't hurt to deliver a note from one friend to another simply requesting a visit. It would do Sonny good to see one of his old friends.*

Assured that she was doing the right thing in delivering the note for Sonny, Caroline turned her thoughts to other things. The talk today with Sonny about values and ideals had made her come to some unsettling conclusions about herself. Up until now, she had lived a completely useless, shallow kind of existence.

"But I'm going to change all that starting right now!" she said aloud, picking up her pace. If she hurried, she'd be able to talk to Dr. Keenan about tutoring more inmates before meeting Chrissy at the Rocky Mountain Club.

She was walking toward the sociology department when she heard somebody calling her name. She turned to see Robert Winston hurrying toward her, his gold-rimmed glasses gleaming in the sunlight. Caroline felt a brief tinge of embarrassment as she watched Robert approaching her. She hadn't seen Robert since the day after she and Chrissy had returned from Fort Collins. She'd told him bluntly that his letter had been the cause of her breakup with Luke, and if she couldn't have Luke, she didn't want anyone. Robert had been so taken aback by her outburst that he'd stammered an apology and quickly disappeared.

"Hi, Cara." Robert stopped in front of her now and adjusted his wire-rimmed glasses with one finger.

"Hi, Robert," Caroline replied, feeling rather awkward.

"Where are you headed?" Robert asked with a smile.

"I was just on my way to the sociology building," Caroline explained.

"Do you mind if I walk with you?" he asked.

Caroline shook her head and together they began to walk.

"I just want to say again that I'm sorry you and

Luke broke up. I guess you're still pretty upset with me about that letter."

Caroline shrugged. "These things happen." She really didn't want to go into the whole episode again. It was much better forgotten.

"I lied," Robert said suddenly, making Caroline stop walking and look at him in surprise. "I lied when I said I was sorry. I'm not sorry that you and Luke broke up." He pushed a strand of his brown hair off his forehead and looked at her intently. "Cara, I know you said you didn't want to go out with me anymore, but I wondered if maybe you've changed your mind since then. Is there a chance that you and I can pick up where we left off? I'd really like to go out with you again."

Caroline looked at Robert. He was wearing the same tweed jacket with the suede patches on the elbows that he had worn the first time she'd met him at the Music Society meeting. He looked very mature, with an understated elegance that came from being raised in a privileged background. He was everything she would have wanted in a boyfriend at one time. *But I've changed,* Caroline thought to herself. *I've gone through a major transition in the last few weeks.* She shook her head and looked at him sadly. "No Robert, I don't think we can pick up where we left off. It just wouldn't work between us."

"Can I ask why?" Robert looked at her curiously.

Caroline sighed. She really didn't want to get

into this, but Robert deserved some sort of an answer. "In the past few weeks my life has taken a different direction," she began. "And I'm afraid that direction is in direct contrast to your lifestyle," Caroline explained.

"I'm not sure I understand," Robert said, his confusion evident on his handsome face. "What am I doing wrong?"

"It's not exactly something you're doing wrong," Caroline said gently. "It's just that we have different values, Robert."

Robert looked at her helplessly. "Is there anything I can say to change your mind?"

"No," Caroline said with certainty.

"Will you let me know if you change your mind?" Robert persisted.

Caroline nodded. "I promise you'll be the first to know."

"Can we at least still be friends?" Robert asked, once again pushing an errant strand of his hair off his forehead.

"I'd like that." Caroline smiled at him.

"I've got to run. I've got a music appreciation class beginning in five minutes." He smiled. "I'll see you later, okay?"

"Okay." Caroline waved as he jogged off in the direction of the music building.

"Well, well, well, if it isn't my old roommate up to her old tricks!" A smug voice spoke from behind Caroline. She turned to see Ellis standing behind her. "Still trying to get your claws hooked into Robert?"

"Oh, Ellis, why don't you grow up!" Caroline returned impatiently. "Robert and I are friends."

"Yeah, right." Ellis snickered in disbelief. "You know, Caroline, you could have had everything if you hadn't gotten so freaked out about a little gossip. The Music Society is the absolute best club on campus and you blew your chance."

"I look at it as a sudden moment of sanity," Caroline returned heatedly. "My quitting the Music Society was the smartest thing I've ever done in my life."

Ellis laughed, a fake little trill that made Caroline grimace in disgust. "The Music Society is the cream of the crop, the best club with the best kids as members. Now, you're nothing more than another college drudge."

"You know, Ellis, somehow I'd rather be a college drudge than be associated with a group of pseudo-sophisticates like the members of the Music Society," Caroline replied, feeling gratified to see Ellis step back as if she'd been slapped. Without another word, Caroline climbed up the steps of the sociology building and went inside.

Caroline made her way through the crowd of students in the Rocky Mountain Club, sorry that she had agreed to meet Chrissy here. Dr. Keenan had agreed to assign her two more inmates and Caroline suddenly realized how much more work would be involved. *Not that I mind,* she said to herself, immediately spotting Chrissy, who was seated at a table in the middle of the room, surrounded by a bunch of kids.

"Come on, Chrissy, give us a hint. What club are you going to show up at next?" a red-haired, freckle-faced boy called to Chrissy.

"Yeah, Chrissy, tell us where to expect you next," a blond-haired girl exclaimed.

"I can't do that," Chrissy laughingly protested, obviously enjoying being the center of attention. "Who knows where Campus Chrissy will turn up next, her pen poised to praise or raze a club!" Chrissy said mysteriously, her blue eyes twinkling as her audience laughed appreciatively. Her smile widened as she caught sight of Caroline. "Hey Cara, over here!" She stood up and waved to Caroline. "You guys will have to excuse me. There's my cousin and we have some catching up to do." Chrissy smiled and waved good-bye as the kids drifted off to other tables, leaving her sitting alone.

"Did I interrupt something important?" Caroline asked as she slid into the chair across the table from Chrissy.

"Nah, they were just some of my fans." Chrissy giggled and leaned toward Caroline excitedly. "Oh, Cara, I'm becoming famous around campus. All the kids are talking about my columns." She looked at Caroline eagerly. "Have you read my second column?"

"Uh . . . I've been really busy, Chrissy. I haven't had a chance yet," Caroline admitted.

"Well, it was great!" Chrissy bubbled enthusiastically. "But wait until you read the column next week! I'm really going to give the Political Science Club a piece of my mind!" Chrissy began to tell her about going to the meeting the night before, giggling as she explained about getting her foot stuck in the plant.

As Chrissy talked, Caroline listened in amazement. *How can Chrissy be so childish, hiding behind plants and wearing funny hats?* Caroline thought. *I can't believe she's taking all this column and club stuff so seriously! Why is she wasting her time on such unimportant matters?*

"Anyway, I heard today that all the members of the Political Science Club are trying to get me taken off of the column. But thank goodness I have a lot of fans, and they won't stand for me being thrown off the paper. Cara . . . you aren't even listening to me!" Chrissy exclaimed in a hurt tone, as she noticed the look of distraction on Caroline's face.

"I'm sorry, Chrissy, but I have a lot of important things on my mind," Caroline explained.

"Like what?" Chrissy demanded. Lately it seemed that Caroline was never interested in what Chrissy was doing or what she had to say.

"I've been assigned to work with two more inmates at the prison," Caroline explained.

"Aren't you taking on a little too much?" Chrissy asked worriedly.

"Of course not," Caroline replied defensively. "It just means more work, but I can handle it."

"But what about your schoolwork? When are

you going to find time to study?" Chrissy asked.

"Don't worry about my schoolwork," Caroline replied. "I'll find time to study."

"But what about fun?" Chrissy looked at her cousin searchingly. "When are you going to have time for some fun?"

Caroline smiled at Chrissy patiently. "Helping other people is much more important than fun. So you see, I don't need time for fun."

Chrissy stared at her cousin in utter disbelief. *It's finally happened*, she thought. *Caroline has completely, totally flipped out!*

Chapter 9

For almost a full week, Caroline hesitated taking the note to Sonny's friend. By Friday night, she decided to talk it over with Trouble. The cat now had his very own litter tray in the corner of her closet, and a large cardboard box with a lid that was lined with one of Caroline's coats. The lining not only made the box a comfortable home, but along with the jazz music she played on the radio, it effectively muffled the sound of scratching and meowing when somebody came into her room.

"I don't know what to do, Trouble." Caroline lay back on her bed, the cat curled up on her chest. "I've always played by the rules, and one of the first rules they told me when I started tutoring was not to carry any correspondence for the inmates." Caroline frowned. "It seems like such a silly rule. What's the harm in delivering one silly, little note for Sonny?"

Trouble raised his head and looked at her, but he had no answers to offer. "That's the good thing about you, Trouble," Caroline continued, scratching the cat's white belly. "I can tell you what's on my mind, and you don't try to give me advice, or try to change my mind. You just listen and that's the best kind of friend to have!"

Trouble agreed with a purr.

Caroline picked up the cat and sat up. "Time for you to go to bed and time for me to get to work," Caroline said, placing the cat into the comfort of the lined box.

As Trouble curled up and immediately went to sleep, Caroline looked at her clock and frowned. It was almost midnight, and she still had at least two hours worth of work ahead of her.

"Oh, well," she murmured with a yawn. "It won't be the first time I've burned the midnight oil." In fact, in the past week, she hadn't had more than a couple hours of sleep each night. Since taking on two additional inmates to tutor, she had discovered there weren't enough hours in the day for her to complete the work she felt needed doing.

It wasn't just work that was keeping her awake. During the past week, Caroline had found herself spending a lot of time thinking, contemplating the values she'd been raised with, and questioning her own philosophy of life.

She couldn't believe what a worthless existence she had led up until now. Taking ballet lessons, worrying about clothes, worrying about what people thought of her—she'd been so superficial, so shallow!

"But now I've developed a new philosophy of life," she told the sleeping cat. "From now on, I'm devoting my life to helping others. I'm not going to be so absorbed with myself anymore."

She got up and went to her desk to find the note. Sonny had given it to her almost a week ago, and had never mentioned it again, probably assuming it had been delivered, Caroline figured. But the note had never been far from her mind.

"I don't break rules," Caroline said softly, looking at the address Sonny had written on the front of the folded note. "At least the old Caroline never broke rules," she amended. "But the new Caroline thinks this is a stupid rule. What harm is there in delivering this note?" She stared down at the note in her hand, realizing she had come to a decision. The address on the note was a street clear across town. *Maybe I'll see if Chrissy wants to come with me,* Caroline thought, realizing that she'd hardly seen her cousin in the past week. *Yes, that's what I'll do!*

Decision made, Caroline picked up the phone to call Chrissy.

Chrissy walked purposefully across the campus grounds toward Fielding Hall. It was just a few minutes past eight o'clock, and like all Saturday mornings, the campus was quiet. Normally Chrissy would have stayed in bed for some extra snooze time to catch up from the late nights of studying during the week, but this morning she had a mission. She was going to try to talk some sense into Caroline!

"She's been so weird lately," Chrissy said aloud, recalling the conversation she and Caroline had shared the week before at the Rocky Mountain Club. After Caroline had delivered her bombshell about not finding fun important anymore, she had immediately said she had too much work and couldn't stay and before Chrissy could protest, Caroline had left.

In the past week, Chrissy had only seen her cousin from a distance around campus and hadn't had a chance to talk to her. So she had been pleasantly surprised when Caroline had called her late last night and asked if she wanted to go with her to deliver something.

"I don't know what she has to deliver, or where we are going to make this delivery, but I'm glad to have the chance to spend some time with her. I want to know where her head is at!" Chrissy muttered to herself, fastening the top button of her coat against the cold morning air.

Chrissy hurried up the steps and into Fielding Hall, then walked quietly down the hallway that led to Caroline's room. She knocked softly on Caroline's door, not wanting to wake up anyone in another room so early on a Saturday morning. When there was no answer, she banged a little harder, knowing Caroline had never been an early riser and might possibly still be in bed. "You'd think since she told me to be here at eight o'clock, she'd have the courtesy to be up and ready to go!" Chrissy muttered, knocking louder this time.

She smiled brightly as the door opened, but her smile faltered slightly as Caroline slid out of the room and quickly closed the door behind her.

"Oh, you're not ready," Chrissy exclaimed, smiling brightly once again. "I'll just come in and wait while you change."

"I'm ready," Caroline countered. "Let's go."

Chrissy stared at her cousin in disbelief. Caroline was clad in a pair of worn jeans and an oversized T-shirt, her old, black coat unbuttoned and hanging loosely around her shoulders. Her pale blond hair, usually perfectly styled with barely a strand out of place, was now carelessly pulled back in a thick rubber band. Her face shone, as if it had just been freshly scrubbed, but without a drop of makeup. *This is a joke*, Chrissy thought. *Caroline wouldn't be caught dead in public without her makeup and nice clothes.*

"Yeah, right." Chrissy laughed. "Really, Cara, I don't mind waiting a few minutes for you to finish getting ready."

"Chrissy, will you stop saying that!" Caroline said impatiently. "I told you, I am ready!"

"Since when are you into the *au naturel* look?" Chrissy teased. She wasn't sure what to make of her cousin. On the one hand she expected Cara to burst into laughter and go back into her room to put on her makeup. But on the other hand, her expression looked so stern.

"Since I decided I have much more important things to do besides wasting time primping in front of a mirror like a bubble-headed coed," Caroline answered firmly and began to walk down the hallway. She turned and looked at Chrissy expectantly. "Are you coming with me, or not?"

"I'm coming," Chrissy exclaimed. *Somehow I get the feeling that I've been thrust into the Twilight Zone,* Chrissy thought, hurrying after her cousin.

"Are you going to tell me where we are going?" she asked as the two girls walked across the campus.

"I've got to deliver something across town, so I thought we'd rent a couple of bicycles," Caroline explained.

"Oh wow, that sounds like fun!" Chrissy said exuberantly. "I haven't been on a bicycle for ages, but I've noticed that lots of students use them around the campus." She looked at Caroline curiously, noticing how the bright sunshine made Caroline's face look pale. "What are we delivering across town?"

"It's a note from Sonny to a friend of his," Caroline explained.

"What!" Chrissy stopped in her tracks and looked at her cousin with shock. "You're delivering a note for a criminal?" She hurried to catch up as Caroline continued walking. "What does the note say?"

This time it was Caroline who stopped and looked at Chrissy in shock. "I don't know, I haven't read it!" she exclaimed. "Chrissy, this is Sonny's personal business, not mine!"

"Caroline, it became your business when Sonny asked you to deliver it!" She and Caroline began walking once again. "You could be an accomplice or something," Chrissy said fervently.

"Oh, Chrissy, don't be so dramatic," Caroline scoffed. "Sonny told me it's just a note asking his friend, Jake, to come and visit him."

"And you believe everything this Sonny tells you? Cara, the man is in prison. He's a criminal!" Chrissy emphasized. *Why can't Cara see reason?* she wondered.

"Sonny is a criminal because society made him a criminal!" Caroline turned and looked at Chrissy, her voice strong and passionate with feeling. "Sonny Maxwell was put in prison because he was robbing places to get money to feed his brothers and sisters. Lots of people are in prison because society left them no choice except a life of crime." Caroline was trembling with emotion. "Look around you, Chrissy. Not everyone is as lucky as you and I have been. All of my life I've been taking what life has to offer. Now I've decided it's time to start giving something back. I'm going to do everything in my power to help the inmates in prison get on with their lives and have a fresh start."

As the two cousins came to a stop in front of the bicycle store, Caroline paused and took a deep breath. "Now, I invited you to go with me this morning because you've been complaining that we never spend any time together anymore. But this is important to me, Chrissy, and if you are going to badger me and belittle my efforts, then I don't want your company!"

"Holy mazoly, okay, I won't badger you," Chrissy answered meekly, intimidated by the forcefulness of Caroline's emotions. *Now I know I've definitely entered the Twilight Zone*, she thought to herself, following the girl who looked like her cousin and sounded like her cousin, but certainly didn't think or act like her cousin, into the bicycle shop.

"Are you sure you read the address correctly?" Chrissy asked, climbing off her rented bicycle and putting down the kickstand.

"I thought I had," Caroline answered. She stopped, and set one foot on the ground as she pulled the small, folded note out of her jeans pocket. "Yes, this is the right street. The address should be on the next block." She shoved the note back into her jeans pocket.

"Let's rest here for just a minute," Chrissy suggested, stretching and flexing her legs. They had been riding for nearly an hour, and even though the girls were both fairly athletic, each were feeling the strain of the long bicycle ride.

Chrissy looked around with interest. "Surely that address you have isn't the guy's home address," she said, noticing that they were in the middle of an industrial area that looked like it had been abandoned years earlier.

"Maybe it's Jake's work address," Caroline offered, also studying the boarded-up buildings that surrounded them. "It's kind of sad to see all these perfectly good buildings just standing around empty," Caroline said reflectively.

Chrissy shrugged her shoulders. "It's progress," she said nonchalantly. "Probably all the businesses moved to other, more modern buildings."

"Yes, but don't you see? That's what's wrong with the world—people just move on and leave things behind without any thought." Caroline's blue eyes gleamed with the fire of inner conviction. "These building have just been left behind to decay and fall apart. They could have been donated to charities, and then converted into something useful like job centers or recreation centers for poor children. Don't you think?" She looked at Chrissy intently.

"Well, sure," Chrissy agreed. *Boy, Caroline sure is getting all fired up all of a sudden over this social-reform business,* she thought. *She's gone from tutoring inmates to converting old buildings. Next thing I know she'll be leading a social revolt or having a sit-in on campus.* She grinned in spite of her concern at the mental vision of her shy, conservative cousin wearing a long string of beads and flowers in her hair, shouting into a megaphone like the hippie demonstrators of the sixties.

"What's so funny?" Caroline asked.

"Oh, nothing." Chrissy climbed back on her bicycle. "Let's hurry up and get this note delivered."

"Okay," Caroline agreed, and together the girls pedaled slowly down the street.

"What number are we looking for?" Chrissy asked as they entered the next block.

"One one five oh five," Caroline answered. "There it is, on the right."

They parked their bikes and for a moment stood looking at the abandoned building in front of them.

"Cara, this can't be right," Chrissy said softly. "Nobody works in this building and surely he can't live here."

Caroline studied the note in her hand. "This is the place." She turned and looked at Chrissy. "You know, lots of destitute people live in abandoned buildings." Caroline once again looked at the note in her hand. "I promised Sonny," she murmured and with a determined look on her face, she walked up to the large, wooden door of the building and knocked loudly.

Almost immediately the door swung open and a tall, heavyset man was framed in the doorway.

"Yeah?" the man growled and Chrissy got the impression of a huge grizzly bear.

"Uh . . . I'm looking for Jake," Caroline's voice was a mere whisper.

"I'm Jake," the man grunted.

"Uh . . . I have a note for you from Sonny," Caroline explained.

"Oh yeah?" The man's large face formed a big, broad smile as Caroline handed him the note. "Thanks, I've been wondering when Sonny was going to get in touch with me." Jake quickly scanned the contents of the note. "Would you mind taking a note back to Sonny for me?"

Caroline hesitated, careful not to look at Chrissy, whom she knew would disapprove.

"It will be a while before I can make it to see him," Jake continued. "A note might make him feel better, you know, let him know his good buddy hasn't forgotten all about him."

"Okay," Caroline finally replied, ignoring Chrissy's swift intake of breath.

It wasn't until Jake had given Caroline his note and the girls were back on their bicycles and pedaling back to the campus, that Chrissy exploded.

"Caroline Kirby, what has gotten into you?" she said angrily. "What do you think you're doing getting involved as a courier between two creeps.

"Sonny is not a creep," Caroline protested indignantly. "And I'm sure Jake isn't a creep, either. They're just two men down and out on their luck!"

"What would your parents say if they could see you right now?" Chrissy returned. "You're wearing the oldest clothes you own, and no makeup, and hanging out with criminals. Aunt Edith and Uncle Richard wouldn't even recognize you!"

"My parents are laboring under a false set of ideals, and they're just going to have to realize that my direction in life is different from theirs." Caroline's voice came out firm and strong.

Chrissy stared at her in horror. *Those aren't Cara's words,* she thought. *She's parroting something somebody else said to her. I can't believe she really believes what she's saying!* Chrissy's eyes narrowed as she guessed where that kind of talk had come from. "Is this the way Sonny tells you to think?" she asked.

Caroline's face flushed. "Sonny doesn't tell me what to think. We just discuss important issues and trade ideas." A small smile crossed her face as she thought of Sonny. "He is such a fascinating person to talk to," she said slowly.

"You aren't getting any romantic ideas about this guy, are you?" Chrissy asked suspiciously.

"Well, what if I am?" Caroline answered defiantly. "He's handsome and bright, and so what if he made a mistake? He's paying his dues, and he's going to make something of himself!"

"Holy mazoly, Cara! Listen to yourself! We're talking about a prisoner!" Chrissy squealed in outrage.

"We're talking about a human being," Caroline returned evenly. "Oh Chrissy, Sonny is like nobody I've ever met before. He makes me think, and he talks to me as if I'm an adult. He's made me see a lot of things about myself, things that ought to be changed!"

Chrissy stared at her cousin wordlessly. *What has this guy done to her? She's so vulnerable, and he's messing with her mind, making her question everything that has ever been important to her!*

"Chrissy, I know it's difficult for you to understand all the changes I'm going through," Caroline said, seeing the shocked expression on Chrissy's face. "And I'm really not even asking you to understand. All I'm asking is that you leave me alone and let me live my life the way I see fit." Caroline looked at Chrissy self-righteously. "I've never told you who to date or who to get involved with," she admonished.

"Yeah, but I never wanted to date a criminal before," Chrissy protested.

"Stop thinking of Sonny as a criminal!" Caroline said impatiently. "Think of him as a misguided person who made a mistake." She smiled at Chrissy reassuringly. "I feel happier now than I ever have in my entire life."

Chrissy looked at her cousin searchingly. She wanted to scream and kick, and slap some sense into Caroline, but how could she when Caroline assured her she was happy? She couldn't argue with happiness! "Okay, Cara . . . if you're sure you're really happy," she finally said, but inside she knew she had to do something. She had to find out more about this Sonny Maxwell character.

"Oh, I am happy!" Caroline beamed and braked to a halt in front of the bicycle shop.

Chapter 10

"Chrissy . . . Chrissy Madden!"

Chrissy turned, her blue eyes widening slightly as she saw Ellis Lattimore hurrying toward her. *What does she want,* Chrissy wondered as Ellis approached her with a friendly smile. *She's always treated me like I was lower than bird droppings, so why is she smiling at me like I've suddenly become her best friend?*

"Hello, Ellis," Chrissy said coolly. There was a time when Chrissy had tried to overlook Ellis's snobbery because Ellis was a friend of Caroline's. But now that Cara had finally disowned Ellis as a friend and a roommate, Chrissy felt no reason to hide her dislike of the girl.

"Is that your Campus Chrissy hat?" Ellis asked brightly, pointing to the beige fedora on Chrissy's head. "Everyone has been talking about your column and your chic little hat. It looks positively darling on you," Ellis gushed.

"Give me a break, Ellis," Chrissy said succinctly. "What do you want? I'm sort of in a hurry."

"Oh, are you on your way to an assignment? Everyone on campus is talking about how you hide at club meetings, and everyone is always trying to guess where you'll show up next. I heard that the Literary Club spent twenty minutes searching the room for you before they even began their meeting." Ellis paused a moment and ran a hand through her sleekly styled, short hair. "You've become quite popular with your column."

"Somehow I don't believe you stopped me to ooze goodwill," Chrissy replied dryly, looking Ellis straight in the eye. "Now, are you going to tell me what you want, or not?"

The bright smile on Ellis's face disappeared and she returned Chrissy's steady gaze. "All right, I'm here to invite you to a charity dance the Music Society is holding in two weeks."

Chrissy snorted in disbelief. "Why on earth would I want to attend a function of one of the most useless, meaningless clubs on campus?" she responded honestly.

"That's not true," Ellis protested with a slight flush on her face. "I'll admit, your cousin had a rather bad experience with the Music Society, but that was as much her fault as anyone's." Ellis didn't seem to notice the look of outrage on Chrissy's face and she continued. "Caroline should have known that she would stir up a lot of jealousy with the other female club members by going after Robert Winston. She shouldn't have let a little adverse gossip run her out of the club."

Chrissy started to open her mouth and defend Caroline. After all, the "little adverse gossip" Ellis had mentioned had actually been out-and-out destruction of her cousin's moral reputation, and Ellis herself hadn't lifted a dainty, manicured finger to stop it. *But, what's the point in defending Caroline now?* Chrissy thought. *Caroline is now out of the Music Society and nothing I say is going to make Ellis change her opinion of what happened.*

"So, will you cover our charity dance or not?" Ellis asked impatiently after a moment of silence.

"I really don't know. It depends on what else is going on the same night. Besides, I never make promises about what event I'll be covering," Chrissy explained, equally impatient.

Ellis gave Chrissy a small smile that reminded Chrissy of the classic evil woman in a TV soap opera. "I just hope you won't let Caroline's little experience with the Music Society color your perceptions of us. After all, a really good investigative reporter would never allow personal feelings to enter into the decision of what stories to write.'

"Point taken," Chrissy said. "Now, if you'll excuse me, I do have important work to do."

With this, Chrissy turned and walked away.

Imagine the nerve of her, Chrissy thought with amazement as she walked toward the south end of the campus. *She came up to me smiling like she was my very best friend in the whole world, and all because she wanted me to cover some charity dance for the Music Society. I can't stand people like Ellis. They're so nice to your face if they want something from you, but they'd think nothing of stabbing you in the back if they don't need you.*

Chrissy dismissed Ellis from her mind and looked at her watch. Darn, she was going to have to hurry. The Astronomy Club would be meeting in an hour, and Chrissy wanted to be in her hiding place well before the meeting got underway.

Chrissy grinned and picked up her pace. She had to admit, the hiding place she had chosen to view the Astronomy Club meeting incognito was really brilliant! She'd hit upon the idea when she had discovered that every two weeks the Astronomy Club met on a hillside on the south side of the campus, just beneath the C.U. water tower.

"This is totally inspired." Chrissy giggled as she reached the hillside and approached the base of the water tower.

"Holy mazoly," she breathed tremulously, looking slowly up the ladder that went up, up, up the side to the small platform that surrounded the tank itself. Chrissy knew this water tank was only a small one compared to most, and from across the campus it hadn't looked so tall. But now, standing at the base and looking up, the tower seemed to reach right up to the sky!

"Maybe this isn't such a good idea after all," Chrissy mumbled, her eyes slowly working back down the tower.

"But, it would be so perfect to write a story about the Astronomy Club while sitting up near the stars," Chrissy argued with the fearful chicken inside her. "It would be the best story you have ever written! Everyone would be talking about it for months!"

"Yeah, but if I've got a broken neck, how am I going to hear everyone singing my praises?" the chicken inside her protested.

"Shut up!" Chrissy told herself sternly. Then, ignoring the internal arguing still going on in her head, she took a deep breath, and grabbed the bottom rung of the ladder.

"Don't look down," she cautioned herself after she had climbed a couple of rungs. "Don't look down because if you do, you're gonna freeze and be stuck on this ladder like a leech against somebody's leg!"

She continued to climb until she reached the small, narrow platform that surrounded the tank, where she collapsed in relief. For a moment she simply sat on the platform, her back against the tank as she relaxed and caught her breath.

The sky had begun to grow dark when she had begun her climb up the ladder, and now the darkness of night had fallen all around her.

Chrissy stood up and looked at the sky, catching her breath at the magnificent view of the stars. The sky was clear and cloudless, making the stars look close enough to reach out and grab in her hand. *The Astronomy Club should hold their meetings up here,* she thought in awe.

"Oh wow," she breathed, focusing her attention down and outward. She could see not only all the lights of the entire campus, but much of Boulder as well. "Even if I don't get a good story on the Astronomy Club, it was worth the climb up here for the view!"

She leaned ever so slightly over the railing and ventured a glance down at the ground beneath her.

"Whoa!" Immediately she straightened up and slapped her back against the water tank, a cold sweat popping out on her forehead beneath the beige fedora. She lay her hands, palms down on the smooth surface of the tank, stroking it for reassurance. *I don't even want to think about how I'm going to get down from here,* she thought nervously. *Why is climbing always so easy going up, but so scary going down?*

Thoughts of her descent left her as she heard voices coming from below. Cautiously Chrissy maneuvered herself onto her tummy and peered over the side of the platform. Her eyes had adjusted to the darkness, and the lights at the base of the water tower gave her a perfect view of two boys struggling to set up a huge telescope.

"Isn't it great that it's such a clear night?" one of the male voices arose to Chrissy. "We should be able to see Piscis Austrinus and Capricornus."

Chrissy frowned, wondering if the guy had suddenly changed over to some sort of foreign language. What in the heck was Piscis whatever and Capricornus? She turned her attention back to the conversation going on at ground level.

"John's supposed to bring the keg of beer, isn't he?" the same voice asked.

"Yeah, he's also supposed to bring a group of girls from Sigma Phi," the other one answered.

"All right!" The first voice hooted enthusiastically. "That's the reason I joined the Astronomy Club. I'd heard lots of rumors about parties under the stars—I can't believe it's for real." Chrissy heard a low chuckle, then the deep voice continued. "I'm into heavenly bodies, but not exactly the kind you find in the sky . . . get my drift?"

"I know exactly what you mean, why do you think I joined the club?" the other voice agreed with a burst of laughter.

Ah, this may prove very interesting, Chrissy thought with excitement. *What a story this will make,* she mused. *I can see the headlines now: Heavenly Bodies in the Sky or Heavenly Bodies Who Party Hardy? What an exposé, a club whose members pretend to be amateur astronomers, but are really just plain old party animals!*

Chrissy's attention returned to the scene on the ground as a pickup truck arrived. As she watched, a dozen girls and guys got out of the truck and within minutes a keg appeared and beer began to flow freely.

"I guess the meeting has now come to order," Chrissy remarked dryly as somebody turned on a transistor radio and rock music filled the air.

The telescope is just window dressing, Chrissy thought in amazement, watching the kids laughing and dancing beneath her, the telescope totally ignored. *It's no wonder they use a front like the Astronomy Club. Keg parties aren't allowed at C.U.*

She wouldn't snitch on the Astronomy Club— instead she'd write the article about an anonymous club, but that way the Astronomy Club would be warned that she was onto them.

Chrissy fumbled in her coat pocket and pulled out her notebook and her pen. She wanted to write down all her thoughts and ideas right now, while she was experiencing them.

"Oops . . ." the pen accidently flew out of her fingers and clattered to the platform, slipping through the thick grillwork and falling to the ground.

Chrissy stifled the impulse to yell, "bombs away" in warning, hoping the pen hit the ground without hitting somebody on the head. When nobody yelled from below, she breathed a sigh of relief. Closing her notebook, she stuck it back in her coat pocket.

I'll just have to remember everything I wanted to write, she decided, straightening up as she heard the distant sound of sirens. As she listened, the sirens seemed to come closer. She looked out across the campus and saw two police cars, their lights flashing brightly in the darkness of the night, quickly approaching.

"All right! What a story this will make!" Chrissy squealed with excitement. "'Astronomy Club Raided by Campus Police'—what a headline!"

But as Chrissy looked down, she realized she wasn't the only one who had heard the approaching sirens. There was a flurry of activity below her and within seconds, the beer keg, the pickup truck and the kids were gone, leaving only the lonely telescope as testimony that the Astronomy Club had met beneath the water tower.

"Rats," Chrissy exclaimed with disgust. "They all got away." It would have been really exciting if the police had arrived while the party below had been in full swing. "Oh well, it will still make a good story." She watched with interest as the two police cars pulled up directly in front of the water tower. Four officers jumped out of the two cars, and Chrissy's interest turned to bewilderment as they each drew their guns.

"Holy mazoly," Chrissy breathed. Was there something else going on below the water tower, something she couldn't see from up above? *Maybe somebody escaped from the prison and is hiding out beneath the tower*, she thought. "Wow, how exciting!"

Chrissy blinked blindly as a brilliant spotlight suddenly hit her in the face.

"You up there in the water tower," a deep voice

boomed over a loudspeaker. "Come down and put your hands up."

"Holy mazoly!" Chrissy squeaked in shock. "They're not after some escaped convict—they're after me!"

"Just a minute!" Caroline jumped and yelled as somebody knocked on her door. "Sorry, Trouble," she whispered, grabbing the cat and putting him in his box. Quickly she placed the lid on the box and shoved it into her closet.

She glanced around the room, noticing for the first time how messy it had become. *When was the last time I straightened up?* she wondered with a frown. She couldn't remember. Lately the days seemed to be running together in a blur. Oh well, she'd get to cleaning up the room later, when she could find the time. She turned up the volume on her radio, then went to answer her door.

"Oh, hi, Connie," she greeted her RA with a tense smile, wondering if somebody had found out about Trouble and that's why Connie was here.

"Hi, Caroline, can I come in?" Connie smiled at her pleasantly.

"Uh . . . sure." Caroline opened the door wider to admit Connie.

"I just thought I'd stop in and see how you're getting along," Connie explained. "You've been in this room a couple of weeks now so I thought I'd see how you like having a single room."

"Oh, I like it fine," Caroline exclaimed, flushing with embarrassment and moving a stack of papers off the desk chair. "Here, have a seat. I'm sorry the place is such a mess, but I haven't had the time to straighten up the past couple of days."

"We never see you down in the lounge anymore," Connie observed, watching Caroline closely.

"Heavens, I'm always too busy to hang out in the lounge. I'm tutoring at the prison along with my regular classes," Caroline explained, pacing the room with nervous energy.

Please, Trouble, don't knock the lid off your box or make any noise, Caroline prayed. In the past couple of weeks, she had grown so attached to Trouble, he really had become her best friend. But the daily worry of hiding the cat was taking quite a toll on her nerves.

"Are you sure you're feeling all right, Caroline?" Connie asked with a worried expression on her face. "Some of the girls have mentioned that they're a little concerned about you. You look really pale and tired."

"I am tired," Caroline admitted. "But this week has really been a mess. It seems like all my professors are having a contest to see who can give the most homework." She forced a bright smile to her face. "I'll be fine. All I need is a few good nights of sleep."

"Okay, if you're sure there are no other problems," Connie said, standing up and smiling at Caroline. "You know us RAs, we're sort of your mother away from home, and it's our job to worry about the girls in our dorms."

"Well, stop worrying about me. I'm fine," Caroline reassured her as she led Connie to the door.

"Let me know if you ever need anything," Connie said. "And get some sleep!" she added firmly.

"Okay," Caroline laughed, breathing a deep sigh of relief as Connie waved good-bye and left the room.

Caroline shut the door and immediately went to the closet to pull out the covered box.

"I'm sorry, Trouble," she murmured, lifting the cat out of the box and cuddling him close to her chest. "It doesn't seem fair that you have to be shoved into a box every time somebody knocks on my door. And it doesn't seem fair that everyone won't leave me alone!" She stroked the cat softly. "I'm doing such good, important work, and I'm tired of people telling me they're worried about me. First Chrissy, and now Connie—can't everyone see that I'm a much better person for the work I'm doing? Can't everyone see how happy I am with my new life?" She brushed her cheek with the back of her hand, surprised to discover she was crying, and she didn't even know why.

Chapter 11

Chrissy was sitting on the top bunk in her room. Denise had left a few minutes earlier for a biology lab, and Chrissy had decided to spend the morning catching up on some of her assignments. She had been spending so much time on her column lately, she'd managed to fall a little behind in her class work.

"But I should be able to catch up on everything with a couple hours of concentrated work," she told herself.

She was surrounded by papers and books. To her left was the first five pages of a biology paper that was due in a week. Directly in front of her were study notes for a French test she was having the next day, and on her right were various textbooks and reference books, along with the notes for her next column. "I'm surrounded by work," she mumbled, picking up the biology papers.

"Rats!" she exclaimed as the telephone rang. She looked down at the telephone that sat on a small table next to the bottom bunk. "I'll just ignore it," she muttered, turning her attention back to the biology papers. Denise was the official phone answerer since the telephone was right next to her bed. But Denise wasn't here just now and Chrissy didn't want to crawl all over her papers just to answer the stupid phone.

"It's probably nobody important," she decided as the phone rang a second time, trying to concentrate on the papers in her hand.

"Oh, double rats!" she exclaimed with disgust. "My curiosity will kill me if I don't answer that!" Deciding not to crawl over her papers to the ladder at the foot of the bed, she leaned over the edge of the bunk. *Surely I can reach the phone from here,* she thought as the phone rang for a third time.

She stretched out her arm, leaning over just a little bit more. "Come on, Chrissy, just a couple inches more . . . ." she grunted, dangling the upper portion of her body off the bed. "Oh triple rats!" she yelled suddenly as she felt herself falling out of the top bunk. She slid onto the floor, knocking the phone off the hook and landing upside down with her feet up over her head. She couldn't help giggling as she noticed that the receiver was now laying in perfect position right next to her ear.

"I'd know that giggle anywhere, Chrissy Madden," a male voice spoke from the receiver.

"William!" Chrissy squealed happily, untangling herself and sitting upright. "Oh, William, it's so good to hear your voice!"

William laughed. "It's only been a couple of days since I last spoke with you."

"I know, but so much has happened the last couple of days," Chrissy replied, her heart thudding happily in her chest as she held the phone tighter against her ear. She closed her eyes for a moment, immediately conjuring up the image of William in her mind. She smiled, thinking of his blond hair, his gorgeous gray eyes and the dimple that appeared in his chin whenever he smiled.

"What could happen in a couple of days?" William asked, then he laughed, a deep, comforting sound. "Dumb question, huh? Knowing you Chrissy, anything could happen. So tell me all about it."

"Well," I guess the biggest thing that's happened in the last couple of days is my arrest," Chrissy said nonchalantly.

"Your arrest!"

Chrissy giggled at the shock in William's voice. Still giggling, she told him about her night spent spying on the Astronomy Club from the water tower, and how the police had arrived to arrest her. "They handcuffed me and put me in the back of the patrol car. I kept trying to explain to them what I had been doing up in the tower, but they kept telling me that anything I said could be used against me in a court of law." Chrissy laughed again. "I felt like I was in the middle of a television series, you know, like Miami Vice or something."

"So what happened?" William asked.

"Once we got to the station, I talked to the captain and explained to him about the column I wrote. He was really nice, but he gave me a stern lecture about being foolhardy, then he called Professor Pauly to confirm everything I'd told him."

"Was your professor angry with you?" William asked, his amusement evident in his voice.

"No, in fact he was pretty cool about the whole thing. He just said maybe I should keep a check on my enthusiasm and concentrate on the mechanics of writing instead of the thrill of being undercover." Chrissy laughed. "In other words, just write the column and don't do anything stupid!"

"I don't understand, how did the police even know you were up there in the tower?" William asked curiously.

"The captain told me that somebody in one of the nearby houses had seen me silhouetted against the water tower and thought I was a sniper or something."

William chuckled. "I guess I can tell everyone here I'm dating a jailbird. Anyway, I'm glad everything seems to be going so well with your column."

"Oh, it is. In fact, I heard yesterday that a bunch of kids are getting together to start a Chrissy Madden fan club. Can you believe it?" Chrissy's voice reflected her pride.

"I can believe it," William answered in a soft voice. "In fact, I consider myself your number-one fan."

"Oh William," Chrissy breathed, warmed by his words. Just talking to him on the telephone always lifted her spirits.

"Chrissy, not a day goes by that I don't think of you at least a hundred times," William continued, his voice as soft as a caress.

"What? Only a hundred times a day?" Chrissy teased.

"That's about all I can manage between flying and my classes. I wouldn't want to have you on my mind when I'm at the controls of a jet airplane!" William replied. "That would definitely cause an atmospheric disturbance!"

Chrissy laughed heartily, then sighed. "Oh William, I've really missed you!"

"I've missed you, too, Chrissy," William said softly. "So what else is happening? How's Caroline?"

Chrissy sighed, a frown creasing her forehead. "To tell you the truth, I've been sort of worried about her."

"How come?" William asked.

"She's started tutoring a couple of inmates at a nearby prison," Chrissy explained.

"Why should that worry you? It sounds like a really worthwhile thing to do."

"It's more than just the tutoring, I think she's gone a little crazy! She's started questioning her whole upbringing, and her values and everything!"

William laughed. "Chrissy, most kids do that when they get into college. It's part of growing up."

"No, it's more than that. She's gotten really attached to one of the prisoners and I'm beginning to think it's an unhealthy attachment!" Chrissy explained. "But she's totally closed her mind to anything I have to say about this guy, and I think he's not only a criminal, but he's a con man as well!"

William was silent for a moment. "Well, if she won't listen to your concerns, there's really nothing you can do," he replied. "Just be there for her when she needs you."

Chrissy sighed. "I know, but it seems like there should be something I can do to make her see this guy for the turkey he is."

"Funny you should mention turkeys," William said. "The reason I'm calling is to ask you about Thanksgiving. Are you planning to fly back to Iowa to spend the holiday with your family?"

"No, my folks can't afford for me to fly home for the four-day holiday," Chrissy replied truthfully. "Things have been pretty tight financially at home these days. I don't really want to ask for any extras." She paused a moment, recalling how guilty she'd felt in planning to go off to college while her parents were struggling on the farm. "I'm just glad my parents insisted that I go to college now instead of waiting a few years."

"I'll always be grateful for that," William replied.

"Grateful? Why is that?" Chrissy asked in surprise.

"If you hadn't come to college when you did, and if you hadn't visited Fort Collins with your cousin, then you wouldn't have shown up at the party, and we wouldn't have met!"

"I hadn't thought about that," Chrissy replied slowly. "I guess it was sort of destiny that made us meet."

"Destiny, fate, whatever you call it," William exclaimed. "All I know is that I've never felt this way about a girl before. I've told my family all about you, Chrissy, and they want to meet you. So I was wondering if you'd come and spend Thanksgiving with us."

"Oh, William, I'd love to come," Chrissy beamed with pleasure. *Thanksgiving with the Powells,* she thought. *Holy Cow!*

"Great! You know my parents have just moved to that new house outside Fort Collins, so if you take the bus up here like you did before, I'll pick you up at the station," William said. "Chrissy, I've got to go, a bunch of the guys want to use the phone," he continued hurriedly, and Chrissy could hear a bunch of male voices in the background. "Plan on Thanksgiving and I'll talk to you soon. Oh, and invite your cousin to come with you over Thanksgiving. I'll fix her up with my brother. She'd like him, he's a junior at Kansas University . . . gotta go . . . 'bye!"

Chrissy slowly hung up the receiver, knowing she had a stupid grin on her face. "That's what love does to you," she said aloud to the empty room. "It puts a silly grin on you face," she said laughing. "And it makes you talk out loud to yourself!"

Her laughter slowly died and her smile faded as she thought of William's last words. *How can I invite Cara to go with me?* she wondered. *She'll probably dress as if she's going to a funeral and make a speech in defense of turkeys!* Chrissy hadn't seen Caroline at all since they had delivered that note across town and that had been over a week ago. She'd stopped by Cara's room several times over the last week, but her cousin was never there.

"Maybe I should invite her to go with me," Chrissy said throughtfully. "However weird she might be acting at the moment, I can't just abandon my own cousin at Thanksgiving. Besides, I think she needs a break from all that prison junk and Sonny Maxwell." Chrissy's frown deepened. "If William's brother is anything like William, he must be really nice. It will be good for Cara to have a little fun for a change!" Chrissy grinned to herself. "And I'll bet Cara hasn't heard all about my water tower adventure. She'll think that's hysterically funny!"

Decision made, and suddenly anxious to see her cousin, Chrissy jumped up off the floor and grabbed her winter coat, then headed out of her dorm room and toward Fielding Hall.

As she walked across the campus grounds, the late autumn air gave her an unexpected pang of homesickness. When Chrissy had been living with Caroline in San Francisco, the seasons had never affected her very much—one seemed to run into the next without much change. But now as she crunched through the leaves on the ground, Chrissy was reminded of autumn in Iowa. She knew the trees back home would mirror the beauty of the brilliant reds and golds of the trees on campus. And right about this time of year would be making a centerpiece of Indian corn and decorative gourds for the dining room table. Thanksgiving was always such a special time in the Madden household. Not only was food plentiful, with turkey and stuffing and all the trimmings, but love was plentiful as well with all the Madden relatives gathered together for the day.

But, this Thanksgiving will be really special too, even though I won't be home to share the holiday with my own family, she thought as she entered Fielding Hall. *This year I'll be with William and his family on Thanksgiving.* She smiled happily. *Now that is really something to be thankful for!*

Chapter 12

"Hi!" Chrissy said with a bright smile as Caroline answered her knock on the door. But her bright smile quickly turned to a look of horror as Caroline stepped out of the room and into the hallway. Chrissy took a good look at her cousin. "Jeez, Cara, you look horrible!" she blurted out.

"Thanks a lot, Chrissy. It's nice to see you, too!" Caroline said dryly, distractedly running a hand through her hair.

"I'm sorry," Chrissy exclaimed, realizing she'd been too blunt, as usual. "But, seriously, Cara, you don't look so great." Chrissy studied her cousin's appearance worriedly.

She's so pale, Chrissy thought. *And she has such dark circles under her eyes.* "Cara, you look like you're totally exhausted!" Chrissy said honestly.

"Don't be silly," Caroline scoffed with a small, high-pitched laugh. "You're just not used to seeing me without my makeup," she explained.

"Well, maybe that's it," Chrissy said dubiously, but she wasn't convinced by Caroline's explanation. "Are you going to invite me in or do we have to stand out here in the hall and talk?" she asked.

"Oh sure. Come on in," Caroline replied, a surprised look on her face as if she'd never thought about inviting Chrissy into her room.

Inside the room, Chrissy received another shock. *What is happening to my cousin?* she wondered as she stood in the middle of the room and looked around. The bed was unmade and covered with papers and magazines. On the top of the desk, books were stacked haphazardly, and soda cans and candy bar wrappers littered the entire surface.

"I know things are sort of a mess," Caroline said, noticing Chrissy's shocked silence. "But I've been so incredibly busy." She began to pace the room, her blue eyes shining with an unnatural brightness. "I started tutoring two new inmates last week, and one of them is being released in a month. I've spent the last week talking to people at various employment agencies, seeing what sort of jobs will be available for him when he gets out." She walked over to the bed and picked up the notebook. "I've started a notebook charting the jobs that are available to these people once they get out of prison." She quickly thumbed through the pages of the notebook. "What I've discovered is absolutely appalling! A lot of the agencies won't even work with ex-convicts. They don't care that the men have been rehabilitated!"

"Caroline . . ." Chrissy started to protest. She didn't want a lecture on the injustices of the local employment agencies.

Caroline held up one of her hands to still Chrissy's protests. "Chrissy, please just listen. This is really important!"

Chrissy hesitated, then nodded and sat down on the edge of the bed, while Caroline resumed her pacing. "The only jobs that a lot of these agencies will offer ex-convicts are menial jobs for minimum wage. They get jobs flipping hamburgers or picking up trash in a park—it's no wonder so many of them go back to a life of crime!" Her voice rose to an indignant shrill, making Chrissy wince. "I'm sorry," Caroline flushed, closing her eyes momentarily and rubbing her fingers in the center of her forehead. "I just get so upset about all this," she said more calmly, opening her eyes and looking at Chrissy.

"Sure, Cara. But aren't you taking all of this a little too seriously?" Chrissy asked worriedly.

"If I don't take all this seriously, who will?" Caroline exclaimed fervently.

"Well, I have a proposition for you that's just what you need," Chrissy said brightly in an attempt to steer Caroline away from the topic of jobs and convicts.

"What?" Caroline looked at Chrissy curiously.

"William called me this morning and invited me to spend the Thanksgiving holidays with him and his family in Fort Collins!"

"I thought you told me he grew up near St. Louis," Caroline interjected.

"He did, but his family lives in Fort Collins now and he wants me to come and spend the holiday with them. He also invited you, and I really think it would be great if we'd both go together!" Chrissy looked at her cousin expectantly.

"I can't go," Caroline declared. "I have too much work to do here. I can't leave for the holiday."

"Oh come on, Caroline. Surely you can take a couple days off for a little break. It's Thanksgiving! Besides," Chrissy grinned, "you know what they say about all work and no play!"

"Of course, you would say something like that," Caroline said dryly, her hands on her hips as she faced Chrissy. "Because your motto seems to be all play and no work!"

"What are you talking about?" Chrissy's grin faded.

"I'm talking about this!" Caroline picked up the latest copy of the *Campus Times* and threw it on Chrissy's lap. It was the column that chronicled Chrissy's water tower escapade.

"Gee, I'm really surprised you actually managed to read one of my columns." Chrissy couldn't help the sarcasm that crept into her voice. Until now Caroline hadn't shown any interest whatsoever in her column.

"Oh, Chrissy, how can you be so proud of writing such superficial drivel?" Caroline asked. "Why are you wasting your time writing social nonsense?"

Chrissy flushed with the beginning of anger. "It's not all drivel! I stopped the Poli Sci Club from sabotaging a demonstration the Women's Forum had planned. I even got a thank-you note from the Women's Forum! Besides, I enjoy writing my column and lots of people enjoy reading it. Not everyone on campus is obsessed with the saving the world!"

"I'm not obsessed with saving the world," Caroline returned heatedly. "But I do believe in doing whatever I can to help the unfortunate people in that prison. And what's wrong with that?" she challenged Chrissy.

"There's nothing wrong with that, Cara." Chrissy stood up and faced Caroline. "But college is supposed to be a time for having fun, and going to parties and dating! You're not doing any of that. All you do is work, work, work!"

"Contrary to what you believe, Chrissy, college is not just for partying and having a good time. It's a time for reassessing values and setting new goals, a time to discover what you want in your life. College is supposed to be the time to mature and grow up. Some people just do it sooner than others," she finished pointedly.

"Are you saying that I'm immature?" Chrissy asked indignantly.

Caroline sighed. "All I'm saying is that you're wasting your writing talent on that mindless column. There are so many more important issues you should be writing about!"

Chrissy stared at Caroline wordlessly. *I know Cara has a tendency to go overboard whenever she gets involved in something,* Chrissy thought. *But this is getting ridiculous. She's forgotten how to smile. She's forgotten how to have fun! It's worse than the Twilight Zone. I feel like she's become the main character in* The Invasion of the Body Snatchers. *Some alien force has snatched my cousin, and replaced her with a bitter, overworked social worker!*

"Cara, I really think it's important that you get away for a couple of days," Chrissy said softly. "Why don't you come with me to Fort Collins. It will be fun!"

"I don't want to go!" Caroline exploded. "I need to stay here and see my inmates. It's Thanksgiving for them, too, but they don't have very much to be thankful for. Sonny doesn't even have any family here in town to come and see him. I have to stay here!"

Sonny again, Chrissy thought. *Always it's Sonny. What is this guy doing to her?*

Caroline glared at her cousin, her body tense with strain. "Why can't everyone leave me alone! Why can't you leave me alone!"

"Because I'm worried about you!" Chrissy

answered with a rising answer of her own. "You aren't yourself. You haven't been yourself since you started that stupid job at the prison and met this Sonny guy!"

"It's not a stupid job and Sonny has nothing to do with it," Caroline retorted. "I'm happy, so why can't you leave me alone!"

Chrissy studied her critically. "If you're so darned happy, then why don't you ever smile anymore? Why don't you ever laugh?"

Caroline's face flushed brightly. "Chrissy, I think it's time that you leave." She walked stiffly over to the door and opened it. "We really have nothing in common anymore. You're still involved with childish games and fun, and I've grown beyond all that."

Chrissy stomped over to the door and looked at Caroline angrily. "I may still be childish, but you've become an old stick-in-the-mud! There's a difference between being involved in something and being obsessed, and I'd say you are obsessed!" She paused and took a deep breath. "Cara, some change is good, but too much change too quickly is unhealthy, and I'm really worried about you!"

"Stop worrying!" Caroline shrieked, tears of frustration starting to glimmer in her eyes. "I don't want your worry and concern. I just want you to leave me alone and let me live my life my way!" She swiped angrily at a tear with the back of her hand. "This is why I didn't want you to come to C.U., because I knew you'd be looking over my shoulder all the time, watching every move I make. I had that for two years when you lived with us in San Francisco. Well, I don't want it anymore!"

Chrissy stared at Caroline, stricken by her words. She never knew Caroline didn't want her to attend C.U.! Anger suddenly overrode her hurt. "Well, unfortunately, you're stuck with me at C.U. right now, but I promise you, you'll never have to worry about me looking over your shoulder again!" Chrissy's words sounded final. "From now on, you can just pretend you don't have a cousin here on campus, and I'll do the same!" At that, Chrissy stormed out, slamming the door behind her.

Caroline stared at the closed door for a moment, her shoulders slumping forward in defeat. She really hadn't meant to make Chrissy angry, and she hadn't meant to tell Chrissy that the idea of her cousin attending C.U. hadn't exactly thrilled her at first. It had all just sort of slipped out.

She rubbed her fingers over her forehead, where a headache was throbbing dully. She couldn't even remember now exactly what had started the fight with Chrissy. Oh well, it really didn't matter, the end result had been what Caroline wanted. *Chrissy won't be bothering me anymore, questioning my work at the prison and trying to make me quit*, she thought. *That's what I wanted, wasn't it?*

Yes, now you've managed to totally isolate

yourself from everyone who cares about you, a small voice whispered in her brain. *Everyone except Sonny, and he's all that's important anyway*, she decided. This was exactly what she wanted, to be free to continue her work at the prison without having to explain or defend herself to anyone!

She rubbed her forehead again, thinking about everything she planned to do that day. She had promised John, one of the two new inmates she was tutoring, that she would get him some books from the library on cabinetmaking. John was an older man, a carpenter, and he wanted to go into cabinetmaking when he got out. She also needed to contact a couple more employment agencies for Chris, the inmate who would be getting out of prison in a month, and she had promised Sonny she would deliver another note to Jake.

She heard a faint, muffled sound coming from the closet. Trouble! She'd forgotten all about Trouble! She ran to the closet and opened the door.

"Oh, I'm sorry, Trouble," she cried, lifting the cat out of the box. "I almost forgot all about you!" She shivered and cuddled the cat close, trying not to think what would have happened if she hadn't remembered the cat now. She would have spent the whole day out, leaving the cat in his little box all day long. He could have suffocated!

"I've got to get my head together," Caroline murmured to the cat. "I've been so forgetful the last couple of days. I missed two classes this week just because I forgot all about them." Of course, she really didn't mind missing the classes. They didn't have much relevance to the real world anyway.

She set the cat down and poured him a saucer of catfood from the bag she kept in her bottom drawer. As Trouble ate, Caroline sat down on the edge of the bed and thought back over the past couple of weeks.

Chrissy was right that she had changed. "But it's been such a good change," she said aloud. She had become a much better person over the last couple of weeks. Finally she was doing really important things with her life. Sonny told her all the time how much he looked forward to her visits and how much he needed her. It was so wonderful to feel needed. Sure, she was tired a lot of the time, and she seemed to cry much easier than she ever had before, but she was working so much harder than she ever had before. Her work at the prison took up most of every day, then her schoolwork took up much of the nighttime hours. So what if she was only getting a couple of hours of sleep each night and eating mostly junk food because she rarely had time to go to the dining hall to eat. She didn't mind these small sacrifices. It was all worth it. She was working for a better world, and that made everything else seem so trivial.

Chrissy slammed the door of her dorm room, making the walls reverberate with the force.

"Ooooh!" she yelled in frustration, stomping her feet angrily.

"I gather something has upset you," Denise's voice came from the bottom bunk bed.

Chrissy jumped in surprise. "I didn't know you were back," she exclaimed.

"I just got back a few minutes ago," Denise said. "What's made you come in here like a thundercloud?" she asked.

"A certain blond cousin of mine, who from this day on is no longer my friend!" Chrissy said stormily.

"Uh-oh, what happened between you and Caroline?" Denise sat up on the bed and eyed Chrissy curiously. Suddenly all the anger left Chrissy and she looked at her roommate miserably. "Oh Denise, I'm so worried about her." She flopped down on the floor next to Denise's bed. "Have you seen Caroline lately?"

Denise shook her head. "No, I never see her around campus anymore."

"She looks horrible," Chrissy exclaimed. "She's stopped wearing makeup, and her face is all drawn and tense-looking. Her eyes are a sort of pink color and she moves like she's some kind of robot in an overload mode." Chrissy frowned, recalling the way Caroline had paced the room, her movements jerky and frantic. "She's trying to maintain a full day of work at the prison and her full class schedule here."

"It's no wonder she looks horrible," Denise

replied. "She's probably suffering from total exhaustion!"

"Well, anyway, she said some pretty horrible things to me," Chrissy continued, her voice reflecting her hurt. "Basically, she told me to mind my own business and that's exactly what I intend to do!" Chrissy looked at Denise defiantly.

Denise shrugged. "Suit yourself, Chrissy. But I'll tell you right now, if Caroline is as messed up as you think she is, she's headed for a big fall. There's no way she'll be able to maintain the pace she's keeping. She's headed for total burnout." Denise looked at Chrissy intently. "When she finally falls and really needs your help, are you going to be able to turn your back on her?"

"I don't know," Chrissy answered. She was still stung by Caroline's confession that she hadn't wanted her to attend C.U. And anyway, how could she help if Caroline didn't want her to? "I really don't know," she repeated. And she didn't.

Chapter 13

"Oh, Chrissy, we're all so pleased you could come this evening," Ellis greeted Chrissy as she stood at the door of The Howard House Hotel on Friday night. The Howard House was one of the most exclusive hotels in Boulder.

Chrissy nodded, looking around the lobby of the hotel with interest. Actually, she hadn't thought any more about the Music Society's charity dance until Ellis had stopped her yesterday on campus to remind her that the dance was tonight. Still angry with Caroline, and somehow wanting to strike back at her, Chrissy had agreed to attend. Besides, she'd thought with satisfaction, it was sort of nice to be so welcomed by a group who had rejected her before.

"Why did you decide to have this charity

dance here instead of someplace on campus?" Chrissy asked.

"Chrissy," Ellis laughed humorlessly. "We members of the Music Society like to do things differently than the rest of the clubs on campus. The Howard House Hotel is more fitting with our image than any place the campus has to offer." She smiled at Chrissy. "Come on, I'll take you up to the ballroom where the dance is being held."

Chrissy nodded and followed Ellis over to the elevators. She wasn't fooled by Ellis's show of friendliness. *She needs me now,* Chrissy thought cynically. *She and her Music Society friends all want me to write a glowing review of their club, so they'll all be really friendly to me tonight. But once the review appears in the paper, Ellis will go back to ignoring me—which is fine with me,* Chrissy thought with a small smile.

As they waited for the elevator doors to open, Chrissy was grateful she had worn her black formal dress. Although plain and simple, the dress fit her attractively and managed to make her look rather elegant, she thought. Ellis was dressed in a tea-length, blue silk dress with gleaming sapphire and diamond jewelry.

"The proceeds from the dance tonight are going to provide Thanksgiving turkeys for underprivileged families in the area," Ellis explained as the elevator doors slid silently open in front of them.

"How nice," Chrissy murmured, stepping into

the elevator and wondering if Ellis had ever thought of how many turkeys she could buy for the underprivileged with the cost of her dress, let alone her jewelry.

"We charged fifty dollars per couple for the dance, and we sold quite a few tickets," Ellis said, pushing the button that would take them up to the fifteenth floor. "Of course, not all the money we collected will go directly for the turkeys. We had to rent the ballroom and hire a band, then of course there were the caterers and the floral arrangements. But, we are happy to do all this for charity." Ellis smiled again, the smile that always somehow made Chrissy think of a snake about to strike. "The Music Society has done many charitable things and we just felt like it was time for the rest of the campus to know about them. That's why we're so glad you came tonight."

At that moment, the elevator doors slid open and Chrissy and Ellis walked to the doorway of the ballroom.

When Chrissy entered into the ballroom, her first impression was that she was Alice in Wonderland, and she had slid down a rabbit hole and somehow ended up in a land where everything sparkled.

"Here we are," Ellis said leading the way.

"Very nice," Chrissy murmured, hoping her total awe wasn't showing on her face. She had never seen anything like what appeared before her now. The massive crystal chandeliers overhead shone brilliantly, and the highly polished wooden dance floor gleamed. The buffet table on one side of the room was covered with a pristine white tablecloth, and that was covered with fine china, crystal and silverware. The band, a ten piece orchestra, was set up on a small stage at the end of the dance floor, their musical instruments shining in the bright spotlights focused on them.

Even the Music Society members themselves sparkled! The boys of course were dressed in conservative suits and tuxedos, but the girls wore glittery, sequined dresses and rhinestone studded gowns with gold and diamond jewelry.

They all look like they are playing dress-up, Chrissy thought in amusement. *They remind me of when I was a kid and me and my friends would dress up in my mom's clothes and jewelry and have a tea party in the backyard.*

"Paul . . ." Ellis called to a tall boy with shaggy, blond hair who was standing nearby. "Come over here, I'd like you to meet somebody. Paul, this is Chrissy Madden."

Paul nodded thoughtfully. "Madden . . . Madden . . . any relation to the Maddens in southern California, the ones who own all the wineries?"

Chrissy shook her head. "No, I'm from the Maddens in Danbury, Iowa, the ones who own a farm with pigs and cows." She grinned mischevously. "Although my Uncle Homer has been known to get his nose into the homemade elderberry wine on holidays." She stifled a giggle at the shocked look on Paul's face and the flush of embarrassment that suddenly colored Ellis's cheeks. *Serves them right,* Chrissy thought in satisfaction. *It should be against the law for kids to be as stuffy as this crew!*

"Uh . . . if you'll both excuse me . . ." Paul said, looking at Chrissy uncomfortably. He walked over to a small group of kids standing near the bandstand, and Chrissy could tell by the way the kids in the group turned and looked at her that he was probably telling them that she had been raised in a pig sty and had an uncle who was always drunk on moonshine.

Ellis looked at Chrissy. "Would you like me to introduce you to the other members of the club?" she asked hesitantly.

"No, that's okay, I'll just wander around on my own," Chrissy said, not missing the look of relief that crossed Ellis's face.

"Okay, I'll touch base with you later," Ellis said. "Let me know if you need any background material on the Music Society, you know, for your column."

Chrissy nodded absently, gazing around the ballroom with interest. *They sure did rent a big ballroom for this dance,* she thought, noticing that there were only about twenty kids in the huge room. *Ellis said they sold quite a few tickets. Maybe more people will be arriving later,* she decided.

Chrissy wandered over to a group of six kids

who were standing near the buffet table. She
recognized two of them immediately as members of the club that she had met through
Caroline when her cousin had first joined the
Music Society.

"Hello, Will ... Annette." She smiled at the
two she knew, even though she hadn't been
very impressed with them when she had met
them previously. *They're so impressed with
themselves, they don't need anyone else to be
impressed,* she thought, her friendly smile not
wavering.

"Oh ... hello," both Will and Annette murmured vaguely, then resumed their conversation with the others.

"Anyway," Annette continued, "I told Daddy I
simply had to go to the Riviera for the
Thanksgiving holidays. I mean, my tan is totally
fading!" She looked at the group in horror, as if
a fading tan was worse than contracting some
dreadful disease.

"I guess a fading tan is about as bad as getting
a zit on the end of your nose," Chrissy blurted
out, but everyone just looked at her blankly.
Don't these kids have a sense of humor? she
wondered. She cleared her throat. "Uh ... I
understand the dance tonight is being held for
charity," she said.

"Is it?" Will asked with a shrug. "I only came
because I knew that La Maison Rouge was
catering."

"Don't you just adore their hors d'oeuvres?"

one of the other girls gushed enthusiastically. "I just love those little canapes!"

Canapes? Chrissy frowned. She always thought canapes were the tops over beds or over the outside of buildings. Wisely, she decided not to say anything.

"Of course, the catering service at la Maison Rouge is sinfully expensive," Annette said, then smiled regally. "But I think the members of the Music Society are worth it!" There was a murmur of agreement among the others.

Speaking of food, Chrissy thought. *I think I'll try some of the "sinfully expensive, adorable hors d'oeuvres."* She wandered over to the buffet table, her eyes widening in delight.

"Holy mazoly," she breathed, her gaze going from one end of the table to the other. *There is enough food here to feed an army,* she thought in amazement. *They should have just invited all the poor people of Boulder here tonight to eat the stuff on this buffet table, that would have really been charitable!* She grabbed one of the china plates and began to fill it. She wasn't even sure what half the items on the table were, but she wanted to try each and every one.

There were little chicken legs, browned to perfection, giant mushrooms stuffed with cheese and bacon, radishes that looked like flowers, meatballs swimming in sauce, and lots of things Chrissy simply couldn't discern what they were. She picked up a piece of toast that was slathered with brown stuff and topped with a slice of green olive.

"Yummy," she murmured chewing slowly to savor the delicious flavor.

"La Maison Rouge makes great canapes," a male voice spoke from behind her.

"Oh, hi Robert," Chrissy turned and smiled at Robert Winston. "I don't know about the canapes, but these little pieces of toast with the junk on top are delicious!"

Robert smiled in amusement. "Chrissy, those are the canapes."

"Oh . . ." Chrissy felt a blush steal over her face. "Well, I agree, they're great." She grinned brightly.

"So, what do you think of our little soiree?" Robert asked.

"You mean the dance?" Chrissy asked. "It's all right, I guess." She frowned thoughtfully. "It just seems like a contradiction in terms, to spend so much money on a function that's supposed to be for charity."

Robert shrugged in agreement. "That's the way most charity events work. Only about an eighth of the money collected actually makes it's way to the charity in question."

"An eighth!" Chrissy looked at him in horror. "But if they'd have held this dance on campus instead of renting a big ballroom, and if everyone had brought chips and dips instead of having it all catered, think of all the money that would have gone to charity!"

"None," Robert answered, pushing his wire-rimmed glassed up with the tip of one finger.

"None?" Chrissy looked at him in amazement. "What do you mean, none?"

Robert smiled at her patiently. "Look around you, Chrissy. Do you really think these kids would pay anything to attend a dance held some place on campus where the refreshments were chips and dips?" he asked dryly.

Chrissy thought for a moment. "I suppose not," she answered. "But it almost seems scandalous to call this dance a charity function. The only people who really benefit from it are the members of the Music Society who attend." As soon as the words left her mouth, Chrissy's face lit up. *Caroline told me I should be writing about something serious,* she thought. *Even though I'm still mad at Cara, maybe she's right. And what can be more serious than a charity dance where the charity gets almost nothing!* She grinned, realizing that she had just come up with the topic for her next column!

Caroline sat at her window, staring out into the darkness of the night. In the spotlight of the light poles that decorated the campus grounds, she could see several couples, some walking slowly hand in hand, while others sat on benches, their arms wrapped around each other.

"Look at them out there, Trouble," she scoffed. "All wasting their time like they don't have a care in the world."

She scratched the cat's black fur absently. "I used to be like that, going out on dates, and going to dances, never thinking about anything but having fun and belonging to the 'right' crowd of kids on campus."

Caroline noticed one particular couple sitting directly beneath a light pole, the girl's blond hair gleaming and the boy's head bent close to hers. As the boy laughed, something in the way he threw his head back reminded Caroline of Luke. She and Luke used to be able to sit and talk for hours, never running out of things to say.

It's funny, I really haven't thought about Luke since I started tutoring. I've been too busy to think about anything else!

Trouble interrupted her thoughts with a complaining meow, and Caroline realized that she had unintentionally stopped scratching him. She resumed stroking his smooth, black fur, causing him to fill the silence of the room with his purring.

"It's funny," she said again, this time aloud to the cat. "I didn't think it hurt anymore about Luke." But thinking about him now, Caroline still felt the hurt as deeply as ever.

"Who needs it?" she suddenly said defiantly. "I don't need a boyfriend, and I don't need anything but my work. I'm happy spending all my time and energy helping others. I'm happy with my life now!" She swallowed hard. "I'm happy," she repeated, choking on a sob. *For somebody so happy, I sure am doing a lot of crying lately,* she thought as she buried her face in the cat's fur and let the tears flow.

Chapter 14

Caroline sat across the table from Sonny, staring at the note Sonny had just passed to her.

"Sonny, I've delivered three notes to Jake in the past week. I can't take anymore. I haven't felt right about this since I started it," she whispered irritably. Lately, it seemed that Sonny was more concerned in passing notes to Jake than in learning what she was supposed to be teaching him.

"This is the last one, Caroline," Sonny said, his blue eyes shining earnestly. "I promise this is the last one. Everything is all set . . ." He flushed. "I mean, I think I've finally convinced Jake to come and visit me."

"Well, okay, but this is the very last one," Caroline said firmly, not able to sustain her irritation with him. "I guess we don't have time for anything else today," she told him, gathering up the stack of books that were spread out on the table in front of them.

Sonny nodded and smiled at her, the smile that always made Caroline want to blush.

"If we work real hard in the next couple of weeks, you should be able to take your equivalency test before Christmas. Won't that be wonderful?" Caroline said enthusiastically.

Sonny shrugged his broad shoulders. "I'm in no hurry."

"I sent away to several places to get some information on college correspondence courses. That information should be arriving any day now." She looked at Sonny curiously. "You are still interested in taking some college courses, aren't you?"

Sonny shrugged once again. "Sure, why?"

"I don't know, you've seemed sort of preoccupied lately," Caroline said, recalling how tense and on edge Sonny had seemed the past week.

"Caroline, life isn't exactly a bowl of cherries in a place like this," Sonny reminded her. "Everyone in here gets a little on edge around the holidays. I guess it reminds us of what we're all missing."

"Oh, Sonny, I'm sorry." Caroline flushed, feeling contrite that she had even questioned him.

Sonny shook his head to dismiss her apologies. "It's not that I have such great memories of the holidays. In fact, usually the holidays just reminded me and mom of how much we didn't have. We never had a turkey on Thanksgiving. We were lucky if we could afford a small chicken!"

"Christmas must have been devastating," Caroline said softly, her heart aching for the hardships he and his brothers and sisters had endured.

"Yeah, Mom always tried to make us all a little something so we'd each have one present to open on Christmas morning." Sonny looked at Caroline. "I'm sorry, I shouldn't be telling you all this."

"Yes, you should." Caroline reached over and took his hand in hers. "Maybe you need to talk about the bad times."

Sonny looked down at where her small hand rested in his larger one and then smiled at her. "If talking about the bad times will give me the chance to hold your hand, I'll talk about them all the time."

Caroline pulled her hand away from his with a small, self-conscious little laugh. There was something about Sonny that was so appealing, she found herself continually fighting her attraction to him. "Well, the bad times will be behind you soon. Once you get out of here, you can get a good job and give your brothers and sisters a wonderful life." She smiled at him. She was so happy that she'd had a hand in helping him better himself.

This is what life is really all about, she thought. *All the missed classes, the nights of little or no sleep, the missed meals—it's all worth it when I see the results of my work. Sonny will pass his equivalency test, and he'll take some college classes and when he finally gets out of here he'll get a good job and become a valuable member of society. And I had a major hand in the whole process!*

"You're looking extremely pleased about something," Sonny observed with a gentle smile.

Caroline smiled at him warmly. "I'm just so proud of you, Sonny. You've made such wonderful progress."

Sonny grinned, his blue eyes gazing at her intently. "A lot of that is because of you. You're not only a wonderful teacher, Caroline, but you're a wonderful woman, too." He laughed as Caroline blushed hotly. "And you blush prettier than anyone I've ever known." Suddenly Sonny's grin faded and he looked at Caroline seriously. "You know, I have really grown to care about you, not just as a tutor, but as something more . . ." he broke off with an awkward smile. "Well, anyway, I just want to thank you for everything you've done for me."

"You're welcome." Caroline smiled shyly, then gathered up her books as she saw the guard signal that it was time for her to leave. "It's time for me to go. I'll see you tomorrow." She started to leave the table, but paused as Sonny touched her arm.

"Don't forget to give that note to Jake as soon as possible. It's vitally important," he said with an intensity that surprised Caroline. Then he laughed, as if realizing he had spoken too seriously. He raked a hand through his blond hair and smiled at her lazily. "I just really want to get my old buddy in here to visit me. I've missed him like crazy!"

Caroline nodded. "I'll try to get it to him some time this afternoon."

"Thanks, Cara," Sonny said, then Caroline turned and left the recreation room.

She got her purse from the security room, then waited for the matron to buzz her out. When the buzz came, she stepped outside the prison door, a happy smile playing on her lips. She always felt good after she finished a tutoring session, but this morning she felt especially great. Sonny's words of praise and caring had really meant a lot to her and her irritation had disappeared.

She had almost reached the place where she had parked her rented bicycle when a voice called out to her.

"Excuse me . . ."

She turned to see an attractive, well-dressed older woman approaching her. As the woman hurried toward her, Caroline noticed her perfectly styled blond hair, and the expensive looking tailored winter coat she was wearing. Caroline shivered, suddenly realizing that she had forgotten her own coat when she had left the dorm earlier that morning.

"I'm sorry to bother you." The woman smiled and stopped in front of Caroline. "But you wouldn't be Caroline Kirby, would you?"

Caroline looked at the woman in surprise. "Well yes, I'm Caroline Kirby."

"Oh, I'm so glad to finally meet you." The woman's face lit up with pleasure. "Everyone has been talking about the wonderful work you've been doing with some of the inmates. They say you're very committed." Her blue eyes gazed at Caroline in admiration. "It's so nice to know there are still young people willing to extend a hand to help others. And to spend your Saturdays here like this—that's real dedication. A lot of people would just as soon write off the people in here as losers," she said indignantly as she gestured toward the prison, the sunlight reflecting off her huge, diamond ring. "Why, all most of them need is a second chance. And it's people like you who will help them make their way in life."

Caroline flushed with pride. *Is this woman a social worker?* she wondered. *No,* she decided, *social workers don't wear big diamond rings and expensive coats. This woman smells of money with a capital M. Maybe she's a wealthy woman who has a lot of time on her hands and does volunteer work.*

"Do you work here?" she asked the woman finally.

"Heavens no, I don't work here, although I do spend a lot of time at the prison." The woman gave Caroline a sad little smile. "My son is one of the inmates here. I try to come as often as possible to visit him." She shook her head. "To this day

I'm not quite sure how he came to be here. We raised our boy with all the luxuries, everything money could buy." A pained expression crossed her face. "Maybe we gave him too much, made things too easy for him." She laughed self-consciously. "But of course this isn't your problem. I just really wanted to thank you for all the help you've been giving Sonny."

"Sonny?" Caroline looked at the woman blankly.

"Oh, I'm sorry," the woman said. "I haven't even introduced myself properly. I'm Vivien Maxwell—Sonny's mother."

Caroline stared at the woman in horror, her head swimming with confusion. "You . . . you're Sonny's mother?" she asked incredulously.

"Yes, and Sonny has told me all about the help you've been giving him. I really don't know how to thank you." Mrs. Maxwell smiled at her gratefully.

Caroline still couldn't quite comprehend what this woman was telling her. All the things that Sonny had said about his mother came rushing back to her. A poor woman with seven children left by her husband to struggle alone. A woman who could never get away to come and visit him. Was it all a lie? Was everything Sonny had told her nothing more than a bald-faced lie?

"What about your other children?" Caroline asked faintly.

"Oh my, we don't have any other children,"

Mrs. Maxwell answered in surprise. "Sonny is our only child."

Caroline's head began to pound. *Lies, lies, lies! The word echoed in her brain.* It had all been a lie! There had been no starving brothers and sisters, no cold, little siblings relying on Sonny for survival.

"Excuse me, I have to go," Caroline murmured weakly.

"Oh, of course, I'm sure you have other things to do." Mrs. Maxwell smiled brightly. "It was nice to finally meet you, Caroline."

Caroline nodded politely and stacked her books in the basket of the bicycle. *I think I'm going to be sick,* she thought as she climbed on and pushed off down the street with rubbery legs.

As Caroline rode back to her dorm room, she tried to make sense of what she'd just learned, but her head was still pounding and she felt as if she were riding through a nightmare or a movie of someone else's life. So much of what she had come to believe over the last few weeks had come from Sonny. Now she knew that his sob story about fate landing him in prison was a lie. But did that also mean that her new beliefs and values were based on lies as well? She felt as if her whole world was crumbling beneath her feet.

I've got to talk to Chrissy, Caroline thought suddenly. *I need to talk to Chrissy. She'll know just what to say to make me feel better. She'll be able to put this all into the proper prospective.*

Caroline frowned and turned her bicycle down

the bike path that led to the college campus. *I can't talk to Chrissy*, she reminded herself dismally. *Chrissy and I aren't speaking*. Her frown deepened. She couldn't even remember what the fight had been about. *But I know I can't go to Chrissy. She won't want to talk to me.*

Tears began to fill Caroline's eyes as she pulled up in front of her dorm and parked her bicycle. *I just need some time to think,* she decided, barely noticing Connie standing in the dorm lobby as she ran for her room. *I've got to think and sort myself out.*

Once in the haven of her room, Caroline threw herself on the bed, her whole body trembling with exhaustion, both mental and physical. Suddenly she realized how hard she had been pushing herself the last couple of weeks. The strain of hiding Trouble from everyone in the dorm, the exertion of making two and three trips to the prison every day, keeping up with the lesson plans, maintaining her own class schedule—it was no wonder she was exhausted!

She curled up on her bed and rubbed her pounding head. Not even Trouble could comfort her this time, as the tears began to roll down her face. "I wish I could talk to Chrissy," she mumbled, and squeezed her eyes tightly shut. She didn't want to open them for a very long time.

Chapter 15

Chrissy rolled over on her bunk bed and groaned as a shaft of bright sunshine hit her squarely in the eyes. "Oh . . . what time is it?" She leaned over the side of the bed and peered down at the clock radio on the small table below her. "Almost noon!" She sat straight up, ready to climb down from the bunk, then remembered it was Saturday. There were no classes to go to, no club meetings to cover. She had a whole glorious day to relax and enjoy.

She lay back down and grinned to herself. William was supposed to call her this afternoon and finalize the plans for her trip to Fort Collins next week. Oh, she couldn't wait to see him again! She hugged herself with happiness at the thought of spending four wonderful days with him. She wondered what William would say when she told him that Cara wouldn't be coming. Chrissy was still furious with her cousin, but she couldn't help recalling what Denise had said. *If Cara was in for a big fall, would I help her, or would I turn my back on her?* Chrissy asked herself. Part of her thought to heck with Caroline Kirby! *Cara says she didn't want me attending C.U. with her. Now, she can just pretend I don't go to the same college as her,* Chrissy thought defiantly. But the other part of Chrissy kept remembering how many times Caroline had helped her when she'd needed it. *Like the time I wanted to impress a blind date and Caroline spent hours teaching me ballet. Or last month when my political science homework was stolen by The Freshman Stalker of Culver Hall, it was Cara who climbed up to the top of the statue in front of the Student Union to put the cap on his head so I could get my notes back.*

"Who cares?" Chrissy said out loud. "I don't owe Miss Kirby a single thing!" She turned as the door to her room opened and Denise walked in.

"Ah, sleeping beauty is awake!" Denise grinned. "I got up a little after nine and I couldn't believe it when I saw you were still snoozing. Normally you're up with the birds!"

"Normally I get to bed before four o'clock in the morning," Chrissy said, covering a huge yawn with the back of her hand.

"Wow, did the Music Society wing-ding last that long?" Denise remarked.

Chrissy shook her head. "I got home from that around midnight. I guess you didn't hear me over your snoring." She grinned at her roommate.

"Very funny," Denise retorted.

"Anyway," Chrissy continued. "After I came in, I turned on my little study lamp and worked on my next column until four this morning. Wait a minute . . ." Chrissy reached around under the covers of her bed and pulled out a crumpled sheet of paper. "Here it is," she said triumphantly, smoothing down the paper and handing it to Denise.

She watched anxiously as Denise read what she had written. "What do you think?" she asked apprehensively. Chrissy had thought it was good when she had written it, but then that had been at four o'clock in the morning following an incredibly boring party, so she could really use a second opinion.

"Shhh," Denise hissed. "Let me finish." Her eyes widened as she read on.

Nervously, Chrissy sat up and swung her feet over the edge of the bed. "It stinks, doesn't it. I shouldn't have tried to write it so late at night," she said dismally.

"Chrissy, would you please shut up and let me finish reading!" Denise exclaimed impatiently.

"Okay," Chrissy replied, scooting to the edge of the upper bunk, not taking her eyes off Denise.

Finally Denise looked up at Chrissy, her expression totally unreadable.

"What? You hated it. It stinks, doesn't it?"

Chrissy exploded, jumping off the bed and grabbing Denise by the shoulders. "Talk to me, Denise. What do you think? Don't be afraid to hurt my feelings."

"Chrissy, this is really good!" Denise said in awe. "I mean, seriously, this is a fine piece of work. Although it really isn't your usual style."

"I was sort of afraid to write something so serious," Chrissy admitted. "But I figure if this article makes even one club rethink the way it handles charity events, then it's worth it."

"Well, this should definitely make some people think." Denise giggled. "I wouldn't be surprised if the Music Society members all get together and burn you in effigy!"

"Do you think I was too harsh on the Music Society?" Chrissy asked. She didn't know why she cared after the way they acted, but for some reason she did.

Denise looked at the article once again and began to read aloud. "'There is an old saying that charity begins at home, and the Music Society definitely believes that old adage. Their charity functions benefit first, the members of the society who attend, providing expensive food, lavish surroundings, and an abundance of self-important back-patting that does no deserving charity any good whatsoever.'" Denise looked up and grinned at Chrissy. "As they say in the West, 'Them's fightin' words, partner!'"

"It's too late to change anything now. I put the

article into the night drop at the paper, and it's being printed today."

Denise and Chrissy both turned as a knock sounded on their door. "Come in," Chrissy yelled.

"Chrissy Madden?"

Chrissy recognized the girl who entered their room. "Hi, aren't you Connie, the RA over at Fielding Hall? she asked brightly.

Connie nodded. "I was wondering if I could talk to you for a few minutes," she said hesitantly, looking awkwardly at Denise.

"I was just on my way over to the Student Union for a while," Denise said quickly, leaving the two girls alone.

"I wanted to talk about your cousin, Caroline," Connie said once Denise had left the room.

Immediately Chrissy tensed up. "Is something wrong?"

"Well, a bunch of us over at Fielding have been sort of concerned about Caroline." Connie looked at Chrissy worriedly. "She's become so isolated and withdrawn. She never joins us in the lounge anymore, and all she seems to do is work at the prison. When she came in late this morning, she was crying really hard, and she hasn't left her room since then."

"Caroline was crying?" Chrissy asked in astonishment.

Something must have really upset Cara for her to be crying in public, Chrissy thought. *Usually she hides her emotions until she's alone. She let out a sigh of frustration. Of course, with this new-*

personality Caroline Kirby, who knows what she'll do? Chrissy thought ruefully.

Even as angry as she had been with Caroline, Chrissy knew there was no way she could turn her back on her cousin. *This is all Sonny Maxwell's fault,* she thought. *He's the one who talked a lot of baloney to Caroline and made her think so weird. I'd like to find out about that creep!* A smile suddenly crossed her lips as a plan began to formulate in her head. After all, she was an investigative reporter, maybe it was time she put her talents to use! She turned back to Connie.

"Don't worry, I'll take care of everything," she assured her. She grabbed her beige fedora and plopped it on her head. "Campus Chrissy is on the job!"

Chapter 16

"Warden Jeffries will see you in a few minutes," the secretary told Chrissy.

Chrissy smiled faintly. She'd left Connie on campus and had come immediately here to the prison. Somehow, some way, she needed to find out everything she could about Sonny-con man-Maxwell. She needed ammunition, something she could take back to Caroline to make her see sense. And so, she had come to the one person whom she hoped could help. *It's a good thing the Warden's on duty on Saturdays,* she thought as she doodled absently on her notepad.

"Warden Jeffries will see you now." The secretary smiled and motioned for Chrissy to follow her. She led her into a large, private office. "Warden Jeffries, this is Chrissy Madden from the newspaper staff at C.U.," the secretary told the distinguished-looking, white-haired man behind the desk.

"Charles Jeffries," the warden smiled as he shook Chrissy's hand, then motioned her to a chair. "What can I do for you, Ms. Madden?"

"Well . . . uh . . . I'm working on an article for the paper and I'd like to know about the tutoring program some of the inmates are involved in," Chrissy explained, pleased at her quick thinking.

"Ah, the tutoring program has been a valuable rehabilitation tool for many of the inmates," the warden said. "We've had tremendous success in educating inmates who desire a high school diploma as the first step in attaining their new lives."

"Uh . . . can you tell me something about the inmates who are in the program?" Chrissy asked, wondering how to bring up the subject of Sonny Maxwell.

"You mean like a profile of the type of inmates involved?" The warden paused for a moment. "It's difficult to talk specifics. Generally speaking, I'd say the inmates would have a genuine desire to succeed. They aren't the hardened criminals, usually they're the ones who made stupid mistakes and are trying to get on with productive lives."

Chrissy frowned at this. *That's exactly what Caroline told me about Sonny*, she thought. *But I've got a good instinct that there's more to Sonny Maxwell than that.* "Have you had any bad experiences with the tutoring?" Chrissy asked.

The warden grinned. "Is this article you're writing for or against the tutoring program?" he asked.

"I'm not sure." Chrissy laughed, relaxing slightly as she saw his friendly smile. "I think I'd like to make it both for and against, then let the readers make the final decision."

The warden nodded. "A good, journalistic decision," he replied, making Chrissy's smile broaden. "Actually, there are several things against the program. Some of the inmates do not go into the program with the right intentions. Some of them see the program as a way to make outside contacts."

Sonny's notes! Chrissy thought excitedly, knowing now that she was on the right track. Sonny had asked Cara to deliver notes so that he could make outside contact.

"I know a girl at the college who's tutoring an inmate named Sonny Maxwell," Chrissy said, deciding to go all the way and lay the cards on the table. She needed to know about Sonny!

The warden shook his head and frowned. "An unfortunate case," he said.

"What do you mean?" Chrissy leaned forward eagerly.

"Maxwell is a tough nut. He grew up as the only child of very affluent parents. He was given everything a child could want, yet he threw it all away for the thrill of committing crimes."

"Holy mazoly!" Chrissy exclaimed. So everything Sonny had told Caroline had been lies! This was exactly the kind of information Chrissy had needed!

"I beg your pardon?" The warden's white eyebrows climbed on his forehead as he looked at her quizzically.

"Oh . . . uh . . . I just remembered an important deadline I have to meet." Chrissy stood up and held out her hand to the warden. "Thanks, Warden, you've been a lot of help!"

"Certainly, it has been . . . interesting . . ." the warden answered as Chrissy raced out his office door.

I've got to talk to Caroline, Chrissy thought as she half walked, half jogged back to the campus. *This should bring her to her senses! That lying creep Sonny Maxwell,* she fumed as she stomped into Fielding Hall and knocked on Caroline's dorm room door.

"Go away," a hoarse voice called.

"Caroline, open the door. It's me, Chrissy!"

There was a long pause. "The door's open," Caroline replied weakly.

Chrissy opened the door, squinting in the semi-darkness of the room. The curtains at the window were pulled tightly shut, blocking out the sunlight, and Caroline was huddled under the blankets of her bed, only the tip of her blond head showing.

"Sonny Maxwell is a lying, scheming creep!" Chrissy exclaimed, walking across the room and opening the curtains, allowing the sunshine to filter into the room. "And it's time you stop the Mother Theresa act and rejoin the human race!"

"Don't yell at me," Caroline said softly.

"Well, somebody has to yell at you!" Chrissy exclaimed. "You've gone completely off the deep end with all this social-reform junk, and all because of a lying creep!"

"I know Sonny is a liar." Caroline sat up and looked at Chrissy.

Chrissy sucked in her breath in shock at her cousin's appearance. Caroline's face was as white as the sheet beneath her, and her eyes were red and swollen with dark circles below. "What have you been doing to yourself?" she gasped.

"Do I look that bad?" Caroline asked in a tiny voice, running a hand through her tangled hair.

"Do you remember the movie, *The Bride of Frankenstein?*" Chrissy said half-jokingly. "Oh jeez, Cara, I was just kidding," she said hurriedly as Caroline began to cry.

"No, I know I look horrible. I feel horrible!" Caroline said between sobs.

"Well, it's no wonder," Chrissy huffed indignantly. "You haven't just been burning the candle at both ends, you've been burning it in the middle as well!"

"I guess I have been a little crazy lately, haven't I?" Caroline gave Chrissy a sheepish grin, then sighed. "But I really enjoy the work I've been doing at the prison."

"Cara, why must you do everything to an

extreme?" Chrissy asked with a touch of exasperation.

"You're the one who always does things to the extreme, not me," Caroline protested.

Chrissy looked at her in disbelief. "Not much! As I recall, when you were taking ballet lessons, you dieted until you nearly fainted from hunger!"

"That was different," Caroline said with a blush.

"No, it wasn't," Chrissy returned in an even voice. "You go into everything you do wholeheartedly, and a lot of times, that's not bad, but this time it's been pretty self-destructive. It's obvious you haven't been sleeping at all and working much too hard. Cara, you can still do your volunteer work, but don't let it consume your life. You don't have to change your whole personality or wear a bagcloth."

Caroline looked at her in confusion for a moment, then a small giggle escaped her lips. "It's sackcloth, Chrissy, not bagcloth!"

"Whatever," Chrissy scoffed. "The point is, it's all a matter of balance."

Caroline sighed thoughtfully. "I've been a fool, haven't I? It's just been so hard, working so many hours and trying to hide Trouble from everyone."

"Hide Trouble?" Chrissy looked at her with confusion.

"Trouble . . . my cat."

Uh-oh, Chrissy thought worriedly. *This is worse than I thought. Caroline thinks she has a cat named Trouble. This sounds really serious.*

Caroline had to laugh at the expression on Chrissy's face. "No, I haven't gone bonkers," she giggled, getting out of bed and going to the closet. As Chrissy watched, she pulled a box out and took off the lid. "Chrissy, meet Trouble." She reached in and pulled the black cat from the box.

"Oh, Cara, where'd you get him?" Chrissy squealed, kneeling to pet the cat and cooing to him softly.

"He found me outside the prison a couple of weeks ago and I've been hiding him in here ever since. But, I'm going to have to find him a proper home," she said sadly.

"Well why don't you ask the girl who used to live in this room?" Chrissy suggested. "You know the girl who just got married."

Caroline smiled. "That's a great idea, Chrissy! She only moved just off-campus so I could even visit Trouble sometimes." Caroline felt as if one great weight had already been lifted from her shoulders. "Hey, Chrissy, I'm sorry I've been such a jerk to you."

Chrissy shrugged and scratched the cat on his belly. "I'm just glad you've finally come to your senses. I hope you aren't going to tutor Sonny anymore. I didn't like the idea of you delivering that note across town for him!"

"I took several notes across town for him," Caroline admitted. "I have one over on the desk now that Sonny gave me yesterday to take to Jake."

Jumping up from the floor, Chrissy picked up

the note from the desk and began to open it.

"Chrissy, you can't read that. It's Sonny's personal business," Caroline protested.

Chrissy looked at her cousin incredulously. "Cara, this is the guy who lied to you about his own family!"

"Okay, read it." Caroline said after a moment's hesitation. She watched as Chrissy opened the note and began to read. "What?" Caroline asked nervously as she saw Chrissy's eyes getting wider and wider. "Chrissy, what is it?"

"I think this is the plan for a prison escape!" Chrissy exclaimed, looking at Caroline in shock.

"A prison escape?" Caroline echoed. That couldn't be, could it? But after what she'd learned about Sonny this morning, she guessed it was probably true. "Oh, Chrissy, I'm in big trouble!"

"Why are you in trouble?" Chrissy asked.

"I delivered all those notes and now I'm an accessory. They could put me in prison!" Caroline's voice rose to a horrified squeak.

"Nobody is going to prison, especially not you," Chrissy said calmly. "The warden is a personal friend of mine. We'll just go talk to him." She smiled at Caroline reassuringly. "We have nothing to worry about."

Caroline looked at her cousin dubiously. "It always worries me when you tell me there is nothing to worry about. Every time you say that, something really drastic happens to us!"

"Look at it this way," Chrissy grinned. "The worst that will happen is that we'll both end up behind bars. But at least we'll be together!" She laughed merrily, but Caroline only groaned in despair.

Chapter 17

"So, is this another reporter on the school newspaper?" Warden Jeffries asked as Chrissy and Caroline both sat down facing him in his office.

"No, this is my cousin, Caroline Kirby," Chrissy explained. "We have a little problem we'd like to discuss with you. Go ahead, Cara."

Caroline flushed as the warden looked at her curiously. "Well, I've been tutoring Sonny Maxwell, and you see, Sonny told me some things that . . ."

"What Caroline is trying to say," Chrissy interrupted, "is that Sonny Maxwell is a big liar." Chrissy leaned forward in her chair and faced the warden earnestly. "You see, Cara started tutoring with the intention of doing something really good for society. And when she met Sonny, he made her feel really sorry for him. After all, he seemed so nice, not like a criminal at all."

"Chrissy!" Caroline hissed in embarrassment. It was one thing to admit that she'd been taken in by Sonny and done something stupid, it was quite another thing to make it sound as if she'd had a crush on him or something. Picturing his blue eyes right now made her want to gag. *I'll never be so gullible as long as I live,* she vowed.

"Anyway, Cara was feeling really bad," Chrissy went on, "and then she started tutoring Sonny and he started filling her head with all kinds of garbage."

"Chrissy, I'm sure Warden Jeffries doesn't care to hear about all the details," Caroline protested. She looked at the warden, shame turning her face a pale pink color. "The bottom line is that I delivered some notes to one of Sonny's friends across town. I know I wasn't supposed to, but it seems I've been lacking common sense for the past couple of weeks."

Chrissy snorted. "That the understatement of the year! In the past few weeks you've put me through a combination of *The Twilight Zone* and *Invasion of the Body Snatchers.*"

"Anyway," Caroline continued, trying to ignore her cousin, "I have the last note here with me, and we thought it would be best if you saw it." She handed the note to the warden.

"Hmmm, looks like an escape plan, doesn't it," the warden said, trying to hide a small smile as he looked at Chrissy. "Does all of this have something to do with your earlier visit with me today?"

Chrissy nodded and grinned at him proudly. "I figured I'd do a little undercover work and see what I could dig up on Sonny Maxwell. When you told me what a creep he was, I ran right to Caroline."

"Well, I appreciate you girls bringing in this note. We'll be sure to take the appropriate action." He looked at Caroline. "And I also suggest that you get yourself assigned to another inmate to tutor instead of Sonny Maxwell."

Caroline nodded, and both the girls stood up, realizing their ordeal was over. "Warden Jeffries, thank you for your understanding," Caroline said softly.

"Yeah, thanks, Warden," Chrissy added with a bright grin. She reached across the desk to shake the warden's hand. "And I promise you, I will write that column on the pros and cons of the tutoring program if you'll see me again for another interview."

"I will definitely look forward to it." The warden smiled. "And once again, thank you girls for coming by."

"I'm so glad that's all over." Caroline breathed a sigh of relief as the two girls walked out of the prison.

"I told you everything would be all right," Chrissy said.

"Chrissy," Caroline began hesitantly, "I've been really spacey lately. I know we had a fight the other day, but I really can't remember everything we said." Her pale face flushed darkly. "Anyway, if I said anything to offend you, I'm really sorry."

"You did," Chrissy said stiffly, recalling why she was supposed to be angry with her cousin.

"What did I say?" Caroline asked, her eyes not meeting Chrissy's.

"Just that you didn't want me to come to C.U. with you," Chrissy said tightly.

"Oh . . ." Caroline was silent for a long moment. "It's true, I mean it was true." Caroline's flush deepened. "You see Chrissy, we had just finished spending two years in each other's back pockets in San Francisco, and I wanted a chance to really be on my own. I guess I was afraid that you'd overshadow me in college."

"That's ridiculous," Chrissy scolded.

"No, it's not," Caroline persisted. "Sometimes I think my whole problem is that I identify too closely with you. I mean, I saw you all excited about William and your column, and everything seemed to be going so great for you, it made me realize how empty my life was at the moment. So, when the chance came to tutor, I jumped right in and I guess I went one step too far."

"Are you saying that this is somehow all my fault?" Chrissy asked defensively.

"No, I definitely take the blame this time." Caroline smiled at Chrissy. "What I'm saying is that I'm glad you're here with me now, and I'm glad you're my cousin, but most of all, I'm glad you're my friend."

"Really?" Chrissy looked at her dubiously.

"Cross my heart," Caroline said earnestly. "And as I recall, you made me an invitation about Thanksgiving . . ."

"You mean you'll go with me to visit William and his family?" Chrissy asked eagerly.

"I think it would be good for me to get away from here for a couple of days, and I can't think of anyone I'd rather spend Thanksgiving with than you," Caroline said.

Before Chrissy got a chance to respond, they were both interrupted by a loud yell.

"Chrissy! Chrissy Madden! I want to talk to you!"

"Uh-oh," Chrissy muttered beneath her breath as she saw Ellis Lattimore approaching them.

"How dare you! How dare you print such things about the Music Society!" Ellis exclaimed, her face red with anger as she waved a copy of the latest newspaper in Chrissy's face.

"Why, Ellis, you look positively flustered," Chrissy said, with a barely stifled giggle.

"Flustered!" Ellis squeaked. "I managed to get a copy of your article from the newspaper office, and I must say, I'm furious! Have you read this?" she demanded of Caroline.

Caroline shook her head. "I'm sorry to say I haven't had a chance."

"Read it!" Ellis thrust the sheets of paper into

Caroline's hands. "I just can't believe the editors won't stop the printing presses and pull the story," she raged obvious frustration.

"You know, we used to have a bull back home that flared his nostrils just like you're doing right now, Ellis," Chrissy observed as Caroline read the article.

"Oh . . . ! You are . . . despicable!" Ellis exploded, then turned momentarily and glared at Caroline, who had finished reading the article. "Do you believe that garbage? I should sue you, Chrissy Madden. I should sue you for slander!"

"Ellis, you can't sue for slander when everything in the article is the truth," Caroline shot back.

Ellis stared at Caroline for a moment, as if unable to believe that Caroline would stoop so low as to actually agree with Chrissy. "At one time, Caroline Kirby, I thought you had lots of class, but it's become extremely obvious that you're no better than your country cousin! You two deserve each other!"

Caroline grinned broadly at her ex-roommate. "That's the nicest compliment you've ever given me," she said, throwing an arm around Chrissy's shoulders. "Come on, Chrissy, let's go get a Coke at the Rocky Mountain Club."

Together the two cousins left Ellis standing on the sidewalk and headed toward the Student Union. "Cara, let's not fight anymore, ever."

"Okay, it's a deal," Caroline agreed readily.

"Do you think it's a deal we can keep?" Chrissy asked with a small smile.

"Nah!" they chimed in unison, and both of them burst out laughing.

Here's a sneak preview of *Having a Ball!*, book number twenty in the continuing SUGAR & SPICE series from Ivy Books:

"There's a girl stuck up in the ceiling!" a voice yelled from inside the gym. Beth and Caroline looked at each other in bewilderment.

"What's going on?" Beth asked a boy who had just stepped out of the gymnasium.

"I'm not sure. Some girl volunteered to be hoisted up to the ceiling by a pulley to hang decorations for the Holiday Ball. Then the pulley broke, so now she's stuck up there."

Together Beth and Caroline hurried into the gym, where all previous activity amongst the holiday ball decoration committee volunteers had ceased and everyone stood motionless, their eyes focused upward.

Caroline cringed in horror when she saw Chrissy dangling from a rope at the very peak of the high, sloping ceiling.

"Caroline, what's wrong?" Beth asked as Caroline gasped.

"That's my cousin up there," Caroline whispered. *Why, oh why does Chrissy always manage to make a spectacle of herself?* Caroline wondered, unsure if she should be frightened for her impulsive cousin, or angry at her.

"That's your cousin?" Beth asked, her eyes trained on the girl suspended from the ceiling.

"Yes . . . that's Chrissy," Caroline replied with a deep, sigh. She admitted to herself reluctantly that she'd known the problem must involve Chrissy from the moment they'd heard the shouts.

Chrissy dangled from the end of a rope tied around her waist, admiring the large, mirrored ball she had just hung in the center of the ceiling, above the dance floor. The rope that was tied around her waist was thrown over a beam above her and attached to a large pulley machine on the gym floor. Chrissy hadn't hesitated to volunteer to be hoisted up to hang the mirrored ball. She had total trust in the pulley machine and her fellow students. And, what's more, she was enjoying the attention and having fun. Not only would she have the cutest date at the ball, but she'd be the talk of the ball as well.

"Okay, I'm all done. You can let me down now," Chrissy shouted, startled as her voice echoed all around her. Her breath caught in her throat when she looked down at the floor, several yards below her. "Holy mazoly, I didn't realize I was so high!" She touched the rope around her waist, checking to make sure the knot was secure. She was much higher up in the air than the time when she'd climbed up the campus water tower! She was higher than she'd ever been in her life! "Hey, you guys, get me down from here!" She stared down below, wondering why everyone was gathered together, staring up at her. She'd heard several loud shouts minutes earlier, but hadn't paid any attention to what was happening.

"Just a minute," one of the guys manning the pulley machine yelled back to her. "We've encountered a little problem."

"A problem . . . what kind of problem!" Chrissy yelped, her reaction making her sway to and fro. What had seemed like fun a few minutes ago was now beginning to set her on edge.

"The pulley machine is stuck. Just hang tight and we'll get you down," another guy yelled.

"Easy for you to say," Chrissy muttered. "Meanwhile I'm up here flying around like Peter Pan!" she replied, trying not to panic as she once again noticed how far away the kids on the polished gym floor appeared to be. "Hey, Cara!" she yelled, suddenly spotting her cousin standing near the pulley machine. "Hey, Caroline, do something . . . get me down from here!"

Caroline flushed with embarrassment as several of the kids standing around her turned and looked at her curiously. *Not only has Chrissy made a spectacle of herself, she's also managed to make a spectacle of me,* Caroline thought stormily. But her anger subsided when she suddenly realized that this wasn't one of Chrissy's typical crazy escapades. Chrissy was actually in danger.

Caroline hurried over to the corner of the gym, where several guys were working on the pulley machine. "Uh . . . she's not in any danger of falling, is she?" Caroline asked worriedly.

"Heck no." One of the boys working on the defunct machine flashed her a reassuring smile. "If worse comes to worse, we can lower her manually."

"Well, that's good to hear!" Caroline breathed a sigh of relief.

"Is she a friend of yours?" the boy asked curiously.

"You might say that . . . she's my cousin," Caroline confessed with reddened cheeks.

"Hey, Cara, can't you do something to get me down from here?" Chrissy yelled from overhead. "If I fall, be sure and tell Will my last thoughts were of him!"

Mon dieu, Caroline thought in utter embarrassment. Now she's announcing the sordid details of her love life to the whole gymnasium of Holiday Ball volunteers!

"I don't believe it," Caroline uttered as she heard her cousin begin to squawk loudly. "She's singing 'The Man on the Flying Trapeze'!"

"She's really something else . . ." the boy working on the pulley machine looked up at Chrissy appreciatively.

Oh, she's something else, all right, Caroline thought irritably. *From now on I'll probably be know as the cousin of the girl on the flying trapeze . . . terrific!*

"Most girls would be screaming or crying." the boy continued, "But, she's being so cool! I'd really like to date her"

"Too bad, she's already taken," Caroline said sarcastically.

"We've fixed the pulley!" one of the boys exclaimed triumphantly. "Hang tight, we're bringing you down now!" he yelled up to Chrissy, who nodded her head as she clung to the rope around her waist.

"Hey, you guys, take it easy!" she squealed as the rope jerked her sideways. "I think I have two broken ribs!" she complained. "Hey, Cara, look at me! I'm flying!" She kicked her legs wildly and flailed her arms, like some sort of wild bird. Caroline cringed, wishing the floor would open up and swallow her. When Chrissy's feet finally made contact with the gym floor, all the volunteers began to cheer. Chrissy untied the rope from around her waist, then began to bow and curtsy, obviously enjoying the attention.

"You and your cousin are really different," Beth observed.

Caroline grinned at her. "That's the understatement of the year."

"Do you two get along? Do you like each other?" Beth asked curiously.

Caroline thought about the question before answering. Did she really *like* Chrissy? There were certainly times when Chrissy was a test. She could be pushy, loud, impulsive, and downright obnoxious. But, Caroline knew Chrissy could also be fun, caring, and supportive. She looked at Beth with a smile and answered, "Chrissy is the best friend I've ever had in my life."

ABOUT THE AUTHOR

Janet Quin-Harkin is the author of more than forty books for young adults, including the best-selling *Ten-Boy Summer* and *On Our Own*, its sequel series. Ms. Quin-Harkin lives just outside of San Francisco with her husband, three teenage daughters, and one son.